LUCHA

Lucha

A NOVELLA BY CONSTANCE URDANG

COFFEE HOUSE PRESS : : MINNEAPOLIS : : 1986

The publishers thank the National Endowment for the Arts, a federal agency, for a Small Press Assistance Grant that aided in the production of this book.

Cover by Gaylord Schanilee

Calligraphy by Betty Bright

Coffee House Press books are available to bookstores and libraries through our primary distributor: Consortium Book Sales & Distribution, 213 East Fourth Street, Saint Paul, Minnesota 55101. Our books are also available through most other small press distributors, and through all major library jobbers. For personal orders, catalogs or other information, write to: Coffee House Press, Box 10870, Minneapolis, MN 55440.

Library of Congress Cataloging-in-Publication Data:
Urdang, Constance.
    Lucha : A Novella.

    I. Title.
PS3571.R3L8   1986   813'.54   86-20765
ISBN 0-918723-23-4 (ppk. : alkaline paper)

LUCHA

Part I

1

TO THE PASSENGERS on the bus Corceles de la Meseta traveling between the capital and San Luis Potosí in four hours, more or less, once out of the ever-spreading suburbs that ring the city of Mexico there is little to break the monotonous grandeur of the high plains. For most of the journey, the bus traverses a dry upland country, only grudgingly fertile, that runs in scarcely perceptible undulations toward distant mountains the color of twilight. Occasionally some cattle are grazing single file along the dried-up bed of an arroyo. Once or twice a countryman is hurrying his donkeys across the highway with the help of a stout rope and a bundle of twigs that serves as a switch. Now and then the passengers who have not dozed off in their reclining seats, or lost themselves in a newspaper or book, may notice a kind of interruption in the enormous vacancy of the countryside, a house perhaps so intimidated by the vastness of the surrounding country that it does its best to conceal itself. Low, built of mud bricks, roofed with thatch or the broad curved leaves of the maguey cactus, and enclosed by a mud wall or a living fence of organ cactus, its camouflage is perfect.

In such a *ranchecito*, set well back from the main road and reached only by a straggling dirt track over which the Señor Tío hesitated to risk his expensive car, Julia lived where she had grown up with her sister, Luz Filomena, the wife of the Señor Tío.

Inside the house there is a ferment of activity like that inside an ant hill. Evening has fallen, and the men are home from the fields. In the darkening patio with its floor of packed earth, crowded with flowering plants bedded out and in pots, some standing, some hanging from the house wall, the father and his two grown sons are washing themselves at the deep stone trough. The water is cold and black, reflecting one or two early stars. The men splash and blow, sputtering in the chilly evening air. A child runs out of the house bringing a rough towel, and by turns they bury their wet faces in it.

The main room is brightened only by the flickering fire and some candles set on a wooden table; electricity has not yet come to the *ranchecito*, although there is a gas stove. Three other rooms open off the patio; in one of them stands the beautiful bedroom suite from Mexico City that was Luz Filomena's gift to Julia and her husband on her saint's day last year. Now all the family are gathered in the kitchen, the warmth of the fire augmented by so many bodies. Rosario, one of the older brothers, has picked up his guitar. The child Nieves, sitting quietly near the fire, is sleepy and contented. Her stomach is full and her eyes are heavy, but she does not want to leave the warm crowded room to cross the dark patio to her bed. Outside, behind the house, the horses are stamping and muttering, breathing quietly down their noses. A dog barks far away in the hills, and Negrito, the house dog, twitches in his sleep without rousing. Rosario is twanging chords and singing under his breath, *"He, Lupe, Lupita, mi amor…"* His brother knuckles him in the ribs, teasing him about his latest girl.

2

EVEN AS A CHILD, Luz Filomena had always been the lively one, loving music and holding out her little arms to dance. If any of the men were going somewhere, anywhere at all, into the fields to look for a stray goat or lamb, taking the grandmother to early Mass on Sunday, or into town to bargain for seed or weigh the corn, she would beg to go along. And her high spirits made everyone cheerful, even the dour country uncles, their muzzles sprouting gray stubble, who rode silently in the front seat. In the jouncing open back of the truck, Luz Filomena would be laughing and singing, arms spread wide to the blue sky that rose and fell above her as the truck bounded over the road.

When she was old enough, she insisted on going to school, although her brothers had fought against it for years, hiding in the arroyo when the school census taker came, and her sister Julia was happy to stay by the grandmother's fire, learning to shape the tortilla dough into sticky balls and flatten them in the wooden press. Even on cold days, when her shoulders shivered under her thin dress and not even her mother's rebozo, wound twice around her skinny arms and chest, could keep out the wind, she persisted in making the long walk to the schoolhouse. It was an ugly, low, concrete-block building, enclosed by a wire-mesh fence, about three kilometers down the highway. The child stubbornly coveted whatever was waiting inside for her.

As she grew older, everyone agreed that she was the pretty one, with her pale olive skin and her oval face like a peeled almond. Her hair was black and glossy and fell about her shoulders in rippling waves. She still laughed and sang, and whenever she could, she rode in the evening in the rattletrap truck into town. After finishing school in the roadside schoolhouse, she waited at the highway in the chilly pre-dawn air, when one or two burnt-out angels were still hanging in the sky, for the bus to take her to the Secundaria. Julia had left school long ago, and she would marry soon. The brothers, grown, had left the farm. One had gone to an uncle in the capital, one had gone north to try his luck across the border, and one had married a carpenter's daughter in the town. Julia's *novio* was the son of a neighbor, and after the marriage she and her husband would continue to farm the *ranchecito*.

With her certificate from the Secundaria, Luz Filomena determined to work in the town. She was as lively and am-bitious and full of laughter as ever, and her brother who had married the carpenter's daughter gave her a bed in his house. She soon took a job as a combination bookkeeper and stenographer in the office of the most prosperous rug factory in the region. Every Sunday night she dressed care-fully in her fashionable tight dress of a printed synthetic fabric, combed her glossy black hair, made up her face as the foreign magazines had taught her, and walked, smiling, down to the Jardín, where the band played and the young people of the town sat on the wrought-iron benches or strolled arm in arm under the clipped laurel trees. Some of her school friends were here, and Luz Filomena, with her enthusiasm for even the simplest things, was always popu-lar. On Friday evenings she went to the movies, usually with one or two other young girls.

The owner of the rug factory was a short, corpulent young man known to all the employees as El Señor. The son of a wealthy politician, he had never found any diffi-culty in making money. Luz Filomena had been working in the office for about three months before he noticed her, but he soon found out all about her, and within the year they were *novios*. Whatever he had originally intended, the following February, just as the tiny green shoots were poking up through the earth, El Señor and Luz Filomena were married in the Church of the Virgin of Dolores. It was a big wedding, attended by all the relatives on both sides, except for the brother who had crossed the border and was working in Philadelphia. The politician and his fat wife came in their black Mercedes with its pale leather upholstery, and Julia and her husband came in the same dusty, rattling truck that Luz Filomena used to ride into the town as a little girl. Afterward there was a reception at the house of the brother who had married the carpenter's daughter, with plenty of tequila and ice-cold Mexican beer, steaming casseroles of *molé*, white rice, and beans, and heaping platters of salads and fruits.

Luz Filomena was as happy and lively as ever, waving goodbye from the car window as she and El Señor set out on their wedding trip to Playa Azul, and she had not changed when they returned two weeks later. And all the years of her marriage did not change her, although to the sorrow of both families there were no children. If El Señor grew stouter with the years, it was scarcely perceptible, and if he departed more frequently for the capital in his long, expensive car, it was because business, constantly improving, demanded it. Occasionally she accompanied him, twice to the United States for visits of two months or more, but usually Luz Filomena remained at home, overseeing the household and the factory. She still enjoyed going to the movies on Fridays and sitting in the Jardín on Sunday evenings. She even took pleasure walking with her nieces to the sweet-smelling bakery under the enormous stars. On these walks she would often stop at the church to light a candle and kneel for a few minutes at one shrine or another. Although she was not particularly devout, she felt the saints were her friends, and she did not want them to feel she neglected them.

3

WINTER BROUGHT LEAN MONTHS to the little farms on the high plain, for the harvest was never plentiful. Besides their staples of corn, beans, alfalfa, and squash, Julia and Fausto, her husband, cultivated the spiky maguey and fermented its milky juice into the pulque that briefly eases the countryman's life. When times were unusually hard, Fausto and one of his sons would load their three donkeys with sticks and twisted lichen-covered branches of brushwood, or of tough close-textured mesquite, and drive them the long dusty road into the town, where people always wanted firewood. But even wood was not easy to find, and sometimes they spent several days collecting enough for three donkey loads.

And the donkeys had to be fed. Every year, it seemed, there were more hungry mouths. Fausto was still young and Julia was strong and the baby crop never failed. Each new infant was welcomed with all proper ceremony, wrapped in an embroidered white blanket and taken to the church to be presented to the stout, black-robed priest. Afterward there was a little celebration with drinks and cakes, and the drowsy infant itself, unable to hold up its head, would suck a grandfather's offered finger dipped in pulque or tequila.

As the years went by, nine of Julia and Fausto's children survived. A set of twins had been born too soon, and a third child had died at birth, strangled by its own cord. The women said this was Julia's fault, that she had forgotten to think always of the child she was carrying and had carelessly lifted her arms above her head. A fourth child, Agripina Sabina, lived only three years before she was taken, a little angel, to join the company of the saints. This little girl, Julia's third child, had been her aunt Lucha's favorite, light-skinned, black-haired, and always smiling and singing like her. A blossom had sprung from the dry, dusty land of the *ranchecito* from improbable parents. For Julia was as brown and mute as the earth itself, and Fausto was dark and iron-hard like the twisted limbs of the mesquite.

On the day the child died, Fausto made his way, stumbling a little, to the highway. He had to wait a long time before a bus driver took pity on him and slowed down for him to hop aboard, because it was not a regular bus stop and the drivers were not required to take on passengers along the road. In the town, Fausto went first to the carpenter shop of his sister-in-law's father and asked him to make a coffin. By the time it was ready, he had downed a few drinks, and he lurched out into the steep, comfortless street holding under his arm the sad little box with its beveled lid. There was no bus for another hour, so he carried his burden into the nearest bar.

He was the only customer in the shabby bar. Its high walls, from which the dismal green paint was already flaking, seemed to reach up hopelessly toward the dim ceiling. On shelves behind the bar the bottles winked somberly in ambers, sepias, siennas, umbers, viridians, and olive greens. Above the bottles on the right hung the figure of a compassionate Virgin robed in blue, her arms outstretched toward those below. Behind her, mountains, streams, and meadows reached back into a past only vaguely apprehended, and in front of her a reddish votive bulb perpetually glowed. On the opposite wall, in a three-dimensional stein advertising Carta Blanca beer, bubbles rose eternally to the glowing surface and disappeared. A television set at one end of the bar was turned off. By the time Fausto stumbled out, it was evening and the lamps on the street shed a lugubrious light. He had forgotten the coffin, and the bartender rushed out after him, handing it up to him as he teetered on the bus steps and the driver raced his engine.

After the death of Agripina Sabina, life at the *ranchecito* grew harder than before. Two bad years, with scanty rainfall and an unusually cold growing season, forced Julia and Fausto to sell a piece of their land. The old truck always needed repairs, and often they did not have enough money even for a couple of liters of gasoline. But then came a good year, and things seemed to improve. And all the while, good years and bad, new babies were born to them – tiny, dark, monkeylike creatures, all mouth and clawlike hands feebly waving and clutching – and were faithfully carried to the priest.

4

THE CHILD NIEVES woke not gradually but all at once.
The thin morning air was nippy with the night's chill, but
inside the nest of her woolen blanket she was warm enough,
and a bar of sunlight already lay across the doorway. Careful not to wake the others in the room, she disentangled herself from the blanket, shook off the sleep that was sticking
to her like bits of straw, and ran barefoot into the sun, hug-
ging her sweater, a gift from her aunt Lucha, around her
like a rebozo.

She's all legs and long hair, tangled and matted with sleep
and hanging halfway to her waist. Her small face, which
lights up with mischief when she smiles, she keeps half-
hidden, because of a birthmark on her lower left cheek, a
purple raised patch in the shape of a paw print. She has
heard the women talking about it, her mother among them.
Someone said it was the mark of an animal on her. Another
said it was the mark of the Devil. Others whispered that it
meant that her mother had done wrong: the mark was a
sign Nieves was not the child of Fausto.

After hearing the women's gossip, Nieves examined her
face for a long time in the mirror her brothers used for
shaving in the patio. She had never really looked at it before.
Except for the mark, her face was like everyone else's, although darker than some. Could the Devil have marked her
for his own? She had never seen the Devil, and when she
asked her oldest brother if he had seen him, Rosario only
laughed and pulled her hair. That evening she asked her
mother if an animal had been inside the house when she
was born, but Julia, always busy, didn't seem to hear her.

Nieves repeated her question.

"Animals live outdoors, people live in the house," her mother told her, not unkindly. "Nieves, fetch some water in a bowl, now – hurry."

After that, Nieves no longer tried to find out about the Devil's mark on her cheek, but she got into the habit of keeping it covered. Now in the knife-bright sunlight, her long hair hangs forward, keeping the mark in shadow.

How clear the morning is. There is nothing between the girl and the mountains rimming the horizon. A tiny speck of brown earth, made of the same stuff as the stars, part of the universe through which drifts the nebula of Andromeda – what a small speck she is in that huge rolling flatland, like a grain of dust, an insect, a mote dancing in a sunbeam under the immensity of the sky. How many days it takes to walk all that distance to the mountains. For although every year her grandfather makes the pilgrimage to the mountains and beyond, a man can walk only one step at a time. And she knows from the old man, although he did not tell her, that the painful pilgrimage is long, five days and four nights on the road, rising every morning stiff and aching with the cold while the sky is still dark, feet cracked and blistering in the rough sandals, without water to wash in, and with only the cold food carried from home. At one of the stopping places children as big as she die every year, bitten by poisonous spiders. Last year her aunt Lucha went with the pilgrims, but she rode both ways in a bus. The Señor Tío paid.

Sounds from inside the house – the family is stirring. On the hard-packed earth of the back patio, one rooster crows, then the other, and the hens begin their soft gabble. Stamping of hooves, splashing of water, and a muffled clatter of earthenware bowls.

"Nieves!"

With a dirty toe she traces a circle on the ground. The morning-glories have opened, bluer than the sky; near a corner of the house, a monstrously luxuriant morning-glory vine is strangling the tall mesquite. The red geraniums are blooming, and the pink climbing ones as well, strong-scented like the orange and yellow marigolds, flowers of the dead, that her mother has planted along the wall.

"Nieves!"

She would like to stay out here longer, would like to stay here by herself all day, marking the earth with serious patterns traced by a toe, tearing off a morning-glory blossom to suck out its tiny portion of honey, like the last sweet swallow of ice cream sucked through the bottom of the sugary cone, but they are calling because it is time to put on her shoes, wash the night's dreams out of her eyes, pull the brush through the tangles of her hair, and go to school.

Once more the cry: "Nieves!"

She slowly returns to the house.

5

THE TOWN, NOT as large as it appears from the surrounding countryside, spreading out over two hills and filling the gap between, spilling out and seeming to tumble down the steep, crumpled slopes, has a quality of the larger world that the country people recognize and respect. Its houses, some of them built in the old rich colonial days when "society" consisted of mine owners who thought the silver in the hills was inexhaustible, have been remodeled and modernized without destroying the antique façades that give the town so much of its charm.

Tall, cool rooms, floored with tile manufactured in the nearby valley and laid in intricate patterns by workmen taught by their fathers, open onto wide tiled verandas on which the purple-red bougainvillaea, yellow mimosa, mauve wisteria, and vermilion trumpet vine let fall their elaborate festoons like so many colored wax drippings down a tallow candle. Wood is expensive and is used sparingly and with love in the heavy carved doors. Balconies and wrought-iron baroque grilles are all that show from the street, unless a door, briefly ajar, permits a glimpse of a flowering jacaranda and splashing fountains rimmed with fern.

On many of these steep streets crouch the houses of the poor, as they have for two hundred years or more, behind the same soft pink or yellow or blue walls, pockmarked by bullets or the weather, keeping their secrets. Here, though, the rooms are small, and on the walls the bleeding and tormented Christ takes the place of their wealthy neighbors' chic abstracts or many-times-magnified photographs of international rock stars.

Some of these thick anonymous walls protect the complacent middle-class families, in which the old grandma, all in black, still goes to early Mass, in which the stout father, with one or two gold teeth, drives to his office where he sits at a polished desk under his framed diplomas, while the mother drives her own little car to the hairdresser's and to committee meetings of charitable matrons. The children go early to schools run by nuns, the boys with their hair neatly trimmed and slicked down, the girls like little mannequins in their striped pinafores over dull red or dark blue uniforms. And within the houses temporarily vacant except for the daydreaming servants, the sofas and chairs upholstered in crushed rayon velvet and the television cabinets, dining tables, buffets, and china closets in walnut veneer imported from Mexico City stand about awkwardly like guests at a party who have just been introduced to one another.

The town has varied the traditional municipal themes. Possibly because of its odd straddling of the two hills and because one hillside was settled earlier than the other, it boasts two main squares instead of the usual one. The older of these is called the Jardín. In its center, laurel trees pruned in fanciful shapes, their trunks punctiliously whitewashed, edge the quiet flagged paths with their wrought-iron benches. Despite the municipal authorities' efforts, this is the place of the traditional Sunday night promenade. The old Municipal Building is now a museum, but the Church of the Virgin of Dolores opposite, described in the guidebooks as "a miniature gem of colonial church architecture," is the richest and best-loved of the town's six churches. On the third side of the Jardín is a public school, in a fine old colonial building originally a tannery, and on the fourth side are four enormous mansions, now remodeled together into a hotel.

The second square is the Plaza Mayor, and on two sides of

it the new Municipal Building and the big baroque Church of San Policarpo stand shoulder to shoulder. It is pleasant with flowering shrubs and palms, and from an octagonal bandstand in its center emanate the lively and good-natured strains of the Municipal Band on Sunday nights. All the patriotic celebrations are held here, particularly those involving fireworks, since the Municipal Building balconies serve as a reviewing stand for the military and civil authorities, from which they can receive salutes or scatter confetti. The other two sides of the Plaza are simple stone arcades sheltering shops and a couple of cafés whose owners often set up flimsy tables and chairs on the wide sidewalks where people sip lemonade or hot chocolate in the fine star-spangled evenings.

Streets that for centuries were wide enough are now congested with polished foreign cars, ungainly old trucks, and the monstrous silver fleet of the Corceles de la Meseta. Some quarters resound with a constant screaming of brakes, bleating of horns, and thumping of fists on metal. Television antennas have proliferated, lifting bony arms above the picturesque façades like family skeletons that refuse to remain hidden. Under the arcades in the Plaza Mayor, magazines and newspapers in several languages are sold to tourists from all over the world, while in the nearby countryside many grandfathers, and grandmothers too, can't read a word of their native tongue.

Near the market is the street of bars, not the cocktail bars frequented by tourists but drinking places where the country people stop for a few quick ones, which often become many, before boarding the bus for home. These bars have swinging doors like old-time saloons and sometimes the music of a blind singer or a group of traveling instrumentalists. Often, especially on a Saturday night, the doors fly open as a drunk is thrown out onto the street to lie inert, barely breathing, dribbling vomit, a huddle of stiff old clothes, until the police pick him up or, revived by the air and the cold stone, he stumbles away.

The streets of the town are badly lighted. Away from the center, away from the tourists and the hotels and the municipal celebrations, when darkness falls, it is the darkness of a deserted countryside under a scattering of stars broadcast like corn for some celestial fowl. In such darkness, the town's daytime face is tossed aside like a mask. Those who must be in the streets go hurriedly, keeping their eyes on the uneven cobbles, to avoid the crimes of the night: rapes, robberies, bludgeonings, and knifings. Girls, bleeding and crying, have been found by the police and taken to the hospital. Bodies have been found in roadside ditches – once even, it is whispered, a body in a policeman's uniform. No one can know much for certain, for the town publishes no newspaper, and whatever has happened is quickly distorted by worrying tongues.

It isn't easy for a simple person, who only wants to live without making trouble for anyone, to get along in such a complicated world. The town, which values its earlier and more graceful way of life, has been overtaken by the ruthless vans of progress, the reformers in the Municipal Building, the probing antennæ from outer space.

AUNT LUCHA HAS made a generous offer. She wants
Nieves to have a better life, a better education. The concrete-
block schoolhouse on the highway is not good enough. For
one thing, although the federal schools are no longer forbidden to teach religion, they still seem to Luz Filomena
basically godless. For another, the teachers, themselves children of poor families, are sincere but ignorant, bored, and
underpaid. New free schools were built by the revolution,
but the birth rate long ago surpassed their capacity. And
there is a shortage of teachers. How can a man support his
family on a teacher's salary when even a university profes-
sor must hold two or three jobs to make enough money to
live on? Only the least competent teachers stay on in the
rural schools run by the government. The best move along
to teach in normal schools, universities, or the wealthier
private institutions supported by the church. Having traveled with the Señor Tío not only to Mexico City but also
to the United States, Luz Filomena has decided that for her
niece to achieve what she herself could not in spite of all
her striving, Nieves must attend the Instituto Sor Juana Inés
de la Cruz, the town's most exclusive school, run by grim-
faced Dominican sisters. Some of its graduates, even girls,
have gone on to the university. Although uncertain exactly
what she wants for Nieves, Luz Filomena has decided that
the Instituto must be her first step. Furthermore, since her
parents' house, out in the country, is too far from the school,
she has decided that Nieves must live with her in town.
    "She will be like a daughter to me and the Señor Tío,"

she assures Julia. "You know it has always saddened me that we have no children of our own."

Julia nods. "The child is fond of you and the Señor," she says slowly.

"The town is not so far away. You can come whenever you like, and on Saturdays we can bring Nieves for a visit."

It is a clear, chilly day with strong winds. Luz Filomena has driven out to the *ranchecito* ostensibly to buy late honey. Ever since she was a girl, she has been greedy for sweets, and now she can indulge herself. She particularly enjoys taking home a bucketful of the thick translucent syrup still crude, with bits of the hive mixed in and even wings or dead insects, and boiling and skimming it on her new gas range. But it is too late in the season, and the last of the honey has been sold.

The two sisters are sitting in a sunny corner of the patio, out of the wind. The contrast between them is greater than ever. Although she is only a few years older, Julia already has the ageless, antique look of the countrywoman of the high plains. Her weathered skin is a network of tiny wrinkles that will deepen, as her burning eyes sink farther into her skull and the flesh falls away like a mummy's flesh. Her feet, in rough sandals, are filmed over with the purple-gray dust that the wind whirls like tiny tornadoes from the dry fields. Over a shapeless cotton dress she wears a dirty apron and a dull black shawl. Her strong hard hands never stop working, sorting dried beans. Luz Filomena, whose hands are also busy, smoothing and rearranging her lustrous hair, is wearing a tight skirt, a sweater of olive green, and a cerulean shawl twisted around her plump shoulders.

"Schooling is important, even for a girl, if she wants to get something out of life."

"You always felt that way, didn't you, Lucha, even when

we were little girls." Julia has used her sister's childhood nickname, the name that means *struggle*. "You were always a great one for struggling against the world."

"Life is a struggle – *la vida es lucha*," Luz Filomena insists.

"One struggles against it, or it takes one where it wills," Julia agrees.

And in this way it was agreed between the sisters that Nieves would leave the *ranchecito* and live with her aunt.

Part II

1

AT THE FOOT of the Street of the Arches, where it runs
into Santa Catalina near the Señor Tío's house, a once clear-
flowing rocky stream is now clogged with refuse and covered with gray scum from washtub detergents emptied there
by housewives and servants. The garbage truck comes once
a week to collect from the midden under the arches, thor-
oughly scavenged by famished dogs roaming the outskirts
of the town or by pigs driven there to supplement their feed.

On the corner next to the stream and just before it flows
into a natural rock tunnel, where the cobbled street broad-
ens for about ten meters into a tiny plaza, a dark doorway
opens into a little shop selling candy, bottled soda, cold
beer, cigarettes, firecrackers, tea, bouillon cubes, soap, washing soda, wax matches, and other small necessities. The
children of the neighborhood gather here. In front of its
doorstep they bounce balls, twirl ropes, and explode firecrackers. In the spring, boys play marbles and girls jump
rope. Early in the morning the small girls arrive with their
mothers' market bags to buy fresh rolls for breakfast, and
all day it continues. Even during school hours, truants and
toddlers keep the storekeeper's wife busy with demands for
Chiclets, penny candies, and matches. After supper, in the
long cool evenings, older boys lounge against the sepia wall
watching the girls on late errands passing through the stream
of light from the open shop door.

The upper end of the street, where it joins the main road
to the highway, is another gathering place. There boys fire
their slingshots at birds and lizards, and girls pick the sparse
upland flowers. Otherwise the Street of the Arches is as
secretive between its tall pale walls as any other street.

Children forbidden to play near the stream that has become a sewer, where the gardeners from the big houses burn their refuse, sending black choking smoke into the clear air, have a long walk to the park at the lower end of town, with its dusty playgrounds and deserted benches under sad old trees. But even there they run and shout, in school hours and out.

They are all over the town. Whether peddling papers, shining shoes, washing cars, carrying market bags for housewives, or simply playing their games with wary eyes, inscrutable faces, they are everywhere, from those with bare dirty bottoms, scarcely able to walk or wrapped in shawls and carried by slightly larger sisters, to boys old enough to drive a truck and girls who work in the factory.

On patriotic holidays, the schoolchildren parade, each school distinguished by its uniform and led by its proudly stepping band or drums and bugles. The girls of the Instituto Sor Juana Inés de la Cruz march in their dark green blazers and white pleated skirts, the boys in white knitted shirts and trousers of dark green. The students from the Colegio Condesa are dressed in maroon and gold, Fray Maldonado in navy blue, Bernal Díaz in purple and white, and San Agustín in brown with white blouses. Although the federal schools require no uniforms, the children wear satin chest sashes in the red, white, and green of the Republic. And after the schools come the representatives of the sporting clubs: soccer, basketball, baseball, and girls' volleyball. Then come the municipal drum and bugle corps and the Lions and other fraternal orders. Following them are foot soldiers and, last of all, mounted soldiers, most admired by the hundreds of children lining the steep streets, watching, licking ice cream, sucking on oranges, chewing pumpkin seeds and spitting the hulls into the gutter.

2

NOW NIEVES WAKENS in her aunt Lucha's house. She wakes up abruptly as always: one minute, curled into a warm knot like a small animal in a burrow, and the next, ready for what the day will bring. Here in the town she has not only a bed but a room to herself. Her aunt fixed it for her, with rugs on the tiled floor, a table with a lamp, a big varnished wardrobe with mirrors in which she can see herself three times reflected, and a colored picture of the Virgin of Guadalupe, who appeared to the poor Indian and caused roses to spring from the living rock.

Her aunt has bought her the dark green school uniform with its green and white smock, the green blazer and white pleated skirt for special school occasions, and dresses for outside school, shoes in the latest fashion, and a warm jacket. They are all hanging in the wardrobe. Nieves hops out of bed, wearing only a cotton vest and underdrawers, and opens the wardrobe doors to admire them. In the bottom of the wardrobe she has hidden a bag of candy. She fishes out a green gummy square, removes the twist of waxed paper, and stuffs the candy in her mouth. The wrapper she discards on the floor. Chewing vigorously, she looks through the bag and takes out some coins to spend in the little shop on the street corner. Although the shop is already open, it is still too early for her to leave the house. The massive carved street doors, which every night the Señor Tío locks and bolts with heavy wooden beams, have not yet been opened. The farthest Nieves can venture is into the patio, but although it is large, like every patio in the town it is completely surrounded by high walls, and instead of a view of distant twilight-colored mountains she can see only the sleeping house itself and the creeper-covered walls enclosing caged birds and flowering plants. If she looks straight up, she can see the sky, pale now and only beginning to be streaked by vivid salmon, but a glance is enough, and she returns to her room, still chewing her gumdrop.

She sucks on an orange-flavored wafer from the bag in the wardrobe while squatting to look through her drawer of special things: a snapshot of her mother holding the youngest baby, three hair ribbons – red, green, and light blue – a necklace of pink beads given her by her aunt, a tiny bottle of perfume also from Luz Filomena, a blue plastic comb with two broken teeth, and a little plastic purse that the Three Kings brought her last year. The purse is empty, so she puts the coins into it. Glimpsing herself in one of the wardrobe mirrors, she strikes a clowning pose standing on one stiltlike leg, her arms akimbo. She sticks out her tongue and approaches the mirror to examine it, bluish-pink with a big bright-orange spot from her candy. Her hair, still uncombed and hanging over her eyes, she pushes back, and at that moment her aunt comes in.

Even at this hour Luz Filomena is fully dressed, although she has not yet put up her wavy black hair. "What, Nieves, still not dressed!" she says, as the little girl smiles at her.

"I'm getting dressed now, Aunt," Nieves replies and begins to put on her school uniform.

Luz Filomena watches approvingly. The child has been with her for nearly two months now, and there have been no difficulties. After an interview, the Mother Superior accepted Nieves into the fourth grade, and so far the sisters have made no complaints about her conduct or diligence. Although she had passed its forbidding bulk almost daily, Luz Filomena had never been inside the school until she entered it for the interview, her hand clutched damply by Nieves.

Built three hundred years ago of the locally quarried gray stone, the school resembled a fortress, the massive walls reinforced by heavy buttresses. At the front, facing the Street of the Sanctuary, stood a bell tower whose four ancient bells rang out the Glorias of Easter week with such clangorous fervor that everyone in the surrounding blocks put his hands over his ears. The door to the schoolyard, next to the convent proper, was narrow in the thick wall, but the sun shone on the paved expanse inside, and wide windows brought light and airiness into the stony classrooms. Luz Filomena was happy to see that the Mother Superior's office, directly off the schoolyard, was open to all the sun and the dust and the high-pitched cries of the pupils.

"We try to perpetuate here the dedicated scholarship of our illustrious namesake, our country's Tenth Muse," the Mother Superior said through her false teeth. Nieves squeezed her aunt's hand as the precisely formed vowels and consonants continued to fall from the Madre's thin lips. "In the primary division, naturally, the requirements are not so stringent as they must of necessity be in the upper division." There was an enrollment fee, a fee for books and materials, and a uniform fee, as well as the tuition, paid each month in advance. "I will give you this little booklet, and each time you pay, it will be stamped, so."

With Nieves still holding tightly to her hand, Luz Filomena walked out into the street, well satisfied. Sor Juana Inés de la Cruz, Mexico's most famous poet, a woman and a nun — what favorable auspices for Nieves to begin her studies. Little is known about Sor Juana. Against the unremarkable background of colonial literature her mannered but graceful and witty verses gleam like pearls on a dun cloth. Her intellect, her talent, and her refusal to deny them – or let them be diminished by the exploitation of her femininity – have few equals in any century or any country.

But Sor Juana is in the past. Even the day of the interview at the school is in the past now, and here is Nieves, standing on one foot, half-dressed in front of the open wardrobe, with only ten minutes to eat her breakfast and leave for school.

"Nieves, your books, your pencils – where are they? Hurry up, now!"

"I'm hurrying, Aunt," Nieves replies, smiling.

"Give me your hairbrush, then. I'll have to help you."

The bells of the Virgin of Dolores are ringing already for eight o'clock Mass, joined by the bells of San Policarpo, the bells of the Chapel of Loreto and of the Sanctuary, each in its own voice calling, warning, insisting, chiding.

"I'm all ready. I'm going now," Nieves says.

3

WHY IS THERE so much suffering in the world? Why must this workman run when he thinks his back is breaking, with the rough strip of sacking across his forehead supporting the load of bricks and straining the swollen veins in his temples to bursting point? Surely his heart, that poor lump of bluish-red muscle, will burst out of its bony cage, or his lungs will explode with the next painful breath. Even in his pleasures he suffers pain: Nieves has heard him moaning and muttering in his drunken sleep, has seen him falter and stumble and fall heavily in the Street of the Arches on one of his rare holidays.

And these bruised feet, caked with gray dirt in their stiff leather sandals – how much farther can they shuffle the old man along, with his battered green paint-blistered box from which he tries to sell the gaudy jewels of sweet jellies and half-melted ices?

The beggar woman, little more than a bundle of unwashed clothes, with one dreadful hand outstretched, palm up, and her whining cry, "For charity!" – why must she crouch on the stones? Nieves feels sorry even for the shaggy little donkeys waiting with their unblinking eyes in the steep alley, for the famished street dogs, and for the pigs that go screaming and incontinent to the slaughterhouse.

She has been living with her aunt and going to school to the sisters for three years. Almost fourteen years old, she feels herself a woman. A year ago, when her blood flowed for the first time, she ran in panic for Luz Filomena, but her aunt was out somewhere in the town, and old Amparo, one of the maids, found Nieves crouching in a corner with her shawl over her head, like a little animal that has crawled away to hide and die. As soon as she realized what the trouble was, laughing and petting the girl, Amparo brewed a pot of manzanilla tea sweetened with wild honey from the *ranchecito*.

"The pain you feel is the pain of being a woman," she told Nieves. "You are no longer a little girl who runs around with bare feet and uncombed hair." And she showed her what to do when the blood came again.

When Luz Filomena returned, Nieves went to her shyly but no longer afraid. "I am a woman now, like you," she said.

Luz Filomena embraced her. "My poor little girl!"

But Nieves did not understand why her aunt, who was always so lively and happy, should look at her with such a rueful expression.

"Come, we will light a candle at the Virgin of Dolores," said Luz Filomena, but Nieves did not want to go. It seemed to her that something of the greatest importance had taken place, but to go to the church and light a candle would somehow belittle, rather than enhance, that importance.

In the country there had not been much going to the church. Only on the grandest fiesta days to celebrate planting, cultivation, and harvest, did the country people leave the land for the dimly lighted, incense-sweet churches and the crowded, decorated plazas of the town. On Candlemas, for example, the day for the blessing of the seed and the ancient Aztec New Year's Day, the town's main streets and the Plaza Mayor and the Jardín are suddenly brightened with flowering plants in clay pots, square petroleum tins, and rusty tin cans, displayed for sale by the country people who before dawn traveled the dusty roads to celebrate this flowering and earn a few coins, perhaps to kneel briefly on the cool, consecrated stones of the Sanctuary, the Virgin of Dolores, or San Policarpo before the long walk home.

By refusing that day to accompany her aunt, Nieves knew she had disappointed Luz Filomena, but during the following year she disappointed her in a more serious way. For although the sisters gave her good marks in conduct and she was diligent in attendance, school was becoming a burden.

Waking in the dim mornings she would feel her old self, but as soon as she remembered school, her stomach would knot up with nausea. She couldn't eat breakfast, and if, to please her aunt, she took a drink of sweet *atole* or chocolate, it would come up again, sour and hot in the back of her throat, and she would run from the table and vomit.

In the classroom she was plagued with headaches, as if a metal band tightened itself around her temples, and at lunchtime she was again unable to eat. She had twice fainted at school, fighting her way up through layers of blackness to find herself lying on the corridor stones surrounded by round-eyed little girls from one of the lower classes. Two of them, giggling, seemed to point at the Devil's mark on her cheek. She raised her hand to cover it.

"Of course, if you don't eat anything, you will have fainting spells," scolded Luz Filomena.

But Nieves could not eat.

"Don't the sisters treat you kindly? Are they mean to you?"

No, they were patient and kind.

"Then what is it? Do the other girls tease you?"

It was not that, either. How could she explain that just looking at the books' pages made her feel dizzy? Nearly every day the girls were called on in mathematics class, and

Nieves' stomach churned so violently she could hardly stand up. Sometimes the pounding in her head made her unable to hear the question.

"I don't know what to do with you," sighed her aunt. "Maybe a tonic." She brought home a big brown bottle from the druggist's, and Nieves obediently swallowed a spoonful every night at bedtime. For a while, although she still could not eat in the morning and her headaches continued, there was no more fainting.

4

DRUNKENNESS IS SELDOM seen in the country, because
the uneven terrain, with its clumps of thorny vegetation and
arroyos filled with brushwood and the prickly branches of
lichen-covered mesquite to keep the cattle from straying
onto the highway, is good cover for a man, especially if he
is lying down. Although from a distance the land appears
smooth and gently rolling, it is irregular, cracked, and
scarred with fissures and sudden declivities. So a man, sod-
den and befuddled with drink, carrying a soda bottle filled
with the colorless grain alcohol still available at most gro-
cery stores if no member of the police is watching, can stumble to rest on the earth and become invisible, a little heap
of rags, all color bleached out by the sun. A cow or donkey,
grazing nearby, may wander over to sniff at him, but otherwise he can lie undisturbed until, groaning and stretching,
he climbs painfully to his feet again and sets off for home.
Another man, after a fiesta, might be helped home by his
friends, for his wife or his sister to lead him to bed. This
secret life of the countryside persists unnoticed, hidden like
the worm and the snail between the flat gray leaves of the
maguey cactus.

In the town, especially on the street of the bars, drunkenness is a different matter, as if insobriety, like the bright
banners and bunting of a holiday of the revolution, were
something to be flaunted and paraded. Within the swinging
doors of a bar, the sharp smells of stale beer, dried urine,
and unwashed bodies, dirt caked in every fold and wrinkle,
mingle with the heady aromas of brandy and tequila. Especially on holidays and weekends, the bars are crowded with

men whose wages are in their pockets and whose time, for a few hours at least, is their own. During the week they work hard and long, rising under the lash of the chilly pre-dawn wind from the mountains. Breakfast is a cold tortilla with *chiles*, and work is unremitting until dinnertime. Construction workers, building new houses rising behind the ancient walls, carry their loads of bricks, piled into a sack on their backs held by a strip of coarse cloth across their foreheads. Mortar is mixed below in the yard and carried in battered petroleum cans on a shoulder, and timbers are carried awkwardly up the steep, twisting stairs. How many climbs, how many burdens, how many times? Like his ancestors, whose bones lay whitening along the roads to the mines of New Galicia, the worker today is still used as a beast of burden, and the heavier the load he carries, the greater his *machismo*.

As the afternoon wears on and particularly with the coming of the sudden upland evening, the bars become louder, and the music of the radio, the jukebox, or the television is replaced, especially on fiesta nights, with live music, a blind singer accompanied by a fiddle, a group of *mariachis*, or simply male voices raised in song none too clearly enunciated.

By nightfall, the street is littered with drunken men, some sprawled on their backs with their wide-brimmed hats over their faces and with their arms peacefully crossed on their chests, others huddled like grimy, bearded fetuses, faces to the wall. Others half-sit and half-lie where they have fallen, propped against the curbstone, uncertain whether to try to stand or simply to lean their heads forward and let ooze out from between slack lips all that poured into them in the course of the afternoon. And some reel back and forth across the cobbles with a disregard for gravity, the anguished yelps of automobile horns, and the importunings of their women. Some are still singing or laughing or cursing the boss. Some make unintelligible speeches. Some weep. And some have knives. By Sunday morning, the jail cells are always full.

Some drinkers make their way unsteadily up the street of the bars to Santa Catalina and then, turning at the little shop on the corner of the Street of the Arches, collapse on the cobbles and packed earth of the tiny plaza near the house of Luz Filomena and the Señor Tío. Sometimes, long after midnight, one of them mistakes the darkened house and pounds on the massive carved doors. And sometimes one of the maids, awakened by the racket, takes pity on him and lets him in to sleep on a straw mat on the floor of her bedroom until morning. The Señor Tío frowns on this practice, and the maid might lose her job if she were found out, but there can be no harm in such a befuddled toper, and if he were left in the street, he might be arrested or might hurt himself.

5

THE FOREIGNERS, PARTICULARLY the *norteamericanos*, were far from a majority in the town, but they made their presence felt. Since most of them were there without obligations that tied them to schedules, they were much in evidence on the streets during the day. And as they tended to live clustered together, rather than diffused throughout the streets that climbed up and down the two steep hills and the dip in the middle, they became even more visible. The one-day tourists arrived by bus in the Plaza Mayor, ate their lunches in the Hotel Colonial or in the restaurant called the Basket of Flowers in the arcades, bought pottery in the market, photographed San Policarpo, and departed the same evening by bus.

Of the foreign residents, the least visible had lived longest in the town. They had the most money and lived behind the highest and oldest walls. Their maids went to the market for them, and houseboys picked up their mail at the post office. They did not attend parades or fiestas; not even fireworks could lure them out through their tall carved doors, although they might watch from a balcony. They had swimming pools, some of them on roofs so as not to mar their patios or the plantings in their tree-shaded gardens. Most of them drove Mercedes, so that when they did venture into the streets, it was never on foot but always insulated by metal and glass. Other foreigners rented furnished houses, complete with maids and gardeners, for three or four months every winter. They subscribed to *Time* and the *Wall Street Journal* and regularly bought *The News* of Mexico City from the boys who hawked it in the arcades.

The students at the Art Center were less homogeneous than the other foreigners. They were adolescents and retired people, beginners and experienced amateurs, of all incomes and degrees of talent. Some came because the climate had been recommended for their asthma, others because they had known someone who had visited the town, still others because they had seen the Center's brochure: "Live and learn in a charming south-of-the-border colonial setting with a faculty of international reputation. New classes start monthly." These students were the most visible foreigners, strolling through the market and filling their mesh bags with tangerines, mangoes, and sapodillas, visiting the shops, and sitting in the Plaza Mayor or the Jardín. They went to the fiestas and movies, especially on English-language days, and when the weather was warm, they swam, took pictures, rode horses, and entertained themselves in full public view.

They were also, in the opinion of many residents both Mexican and foreign, indirectly responsible for the rising crime rate. If full-grown girls walk around half-naked on their fashionable clogs, wearing short skirts and with no bras under their embroidered peasant blouses, they must expect to be raped. And if people leave expensive cameras, transistors, and miniature television sets in their unlocked cars or apartments, they are inviting burglary. Cash is not often stolen, and the police are skeptical of reports of missing money, since foreigners are notoriously careless about money and seldom seem to know exactly how much they had.

There are drunkards among the foreigners too, but they keep to the hotel cocktail lounges and the Serpiente de Edén, whose clientele is strictly *gringo*. They are not welcome in the cantinas and the dangerous street of the bars near the market.

The Señor Tío, in the course of his business, has met a number of foreigners, and some of them have even become friends, in the slightly uneasy manner of people well-disposed but not quite certain of being understood. Occasionally he and Luz Filomena have been invited for drinks to the houses of semipermanent residents, and they proudly include *norteamericanos* on their guest lists, especially to promote the serapes woven at the factory. The Señor knows how business is done in the United States.

6

HAVING A GOOD HEAD for business and knowing how to get along with all sorts of people, the Señor Tío has made a success of the rug factory. His father's money and government position were no drawback, certainly, but he has made his own prosperity. He hires the finest and most original designers to combine the traditional regional patterns with the newest colors and textures. He has no pretensions to artistic or scientific knowledge, but he knows he must turn out a product superior to the serapes sold by Indians in the market, while competing at the same time with the North American carpet mills. They can make any quantity of broadlooms in synthetic fibers that are virtually indestructible, fireproof, and dyed in fantastic colors with chemicals impervious to light, blight, and insects. Therefore, what he produces is a hand-loomed, custom-designed rug of pure wool, using the traditional dyes brewed by ancient formulas from the wild plants of the region. He has gambled on mass-producing, for a limited market, a serape hitherto available only sporadically and rarely on demand. The factory has no automated machines: the huge looms are still worked by hand. Many of the processes, however, have been borrowed from the United States. His proudest boast is that he is never too proud to learn.

A dozen years ago, when he decided to get married, he thought about marrying a North American girl. He was a much-traveled young man, and, although short and plump, he knew himself attractive to women. There were plenty of foreign girls in the town, and he knew he had a good chance of finding an art student who would be flattered and thrilled at the idea of taking a Mexican husband. She would find him as exotic as he found her. After consideration, however, and after Luz Filomena came to work in the office, he decided against marrying a *gringa*. Even if he found a Catholic, as his mother would require, he had spent enough time in the United States to expect differences, incomprehensibilities, arguments. They all wanted — what was it they wanted, those beautiful larger-than-life girls? His ideal wife was loving, lively, and intelligent, not merely a cook in the kitchen and a bolster in the bed but a modern woman who could understand and soothe his business worries, entertain his guests, and at the same time be the proud mother of his children — not someone continually struggling, like these *gringas*, to be a man.

He had chosen Luz Filomena. And he had chosen well. His one regret was that there were no children, but he had not entirely given up hope. He was pleased when she took her sister Julia's child to live with them, thinking she would feel less lonely while he was at work. She, of course, no longer worked at the office.

"I wouldn't want anyone to think I couldn't support my own family, especially such a small one," he said jokingly. He was sorry he had said it when her eyes showed that she thought he was reproaching her for their childlessness. His mother prayed to the saints for a grandchild, and he suspected Luz Filomena of also praying secretly. Once when he was looking for something fallen behind the wardrobe, he had found a bag filled with dried bulbs, already half-decayed. He suspected she had consulted a *curandera*, but neither of them ever mentioned it. Once or twice she had suggested that they see if a doctor could do something about their barren marriage, but there he put his foot down. That was woman's business. He would have nothing to do with

the matter. If she wanted to go to a doctor, that was her af-
fair. He too had read sensational magazine articles about
the repellent tests for sterility. Some articles suggested that
it might be the husband's fault. No one could impugn his
virility, least of all Luz Filomena! He was too much man
for her. His affection and respect for her were as profound
as ever, but on his trips without her he did not travel alone.
He was too modern to support a *casa chica*, as his father
had done, and he didn't want the emotional involvement
of another household. All he wanted was a little diversion
with an attractive woman, a woman in whose eyes he saw
no shadow of disappointment and on whose lips he felt no
unspoken recriminations.

He wanted to be a good man, and, in the eyes of his
family and the town, he succeeded. His factory was well-
run, with good working conditions and fair wages. For rush
orders and overtime, the workers were paid extra. And he
was generous to his wife and her family, although as the
years went by, he grew too busy to spend as much time at
the *ranchecito* as in the earliest days of their marriage, when
they drove out every few weeks for a picnic or a barbecue
of roast kid.

Those country excursions had been for him, a town dweller,
among the pleasantest experiences of his life. He drove his
luxurious new car over the highway until, at some barely
perceptible landmark, Luz Filomena cried, "Turn here!"
The car's springs were so good they hardly felt the jolting
on the narrow track across the scrubby fields. He was always surprised to catch sight of the house, camouflaged in
the countryside. How vast the shallow bowl of the blue sky,
how distant the low-lying mountains on the horizon, how
fresh the sharp thin air after the odors and heat of the town.
He liked drawing up in a spurt of dust at the dooryard,

amid the children's welcoming cries, as his sister-in-law came hurrying through the doorway, wiping her hands on her apron. He liked the acrid smell of roasting meat on the wood fire with its bluish transparent smoke. And after the meal he liked resting on an old serape, tilting his hat over his eyes as the country people did, listening to the chatter of the women, and smoking one of Fausto's bitter little cigarettes, while the children's shouts rang out over the fields, and flocks of starlings and grackles swooped and whirled above on their way to roost in the trees on the steep hillsides toward the town.

7

ALTHOUGH ONLY THE WISEST old women can discern the adult face in the screwed-up, inscrutable features of the newborn, the adult is implicit in the undeveloped infant face, just as the adult stature is prefigured in the tiny limbs drawn up to the swollen torso. So Nieves at seventeen has grown out of her childish skinniness into her inevitable form, her sharp elbows and ankles rounded, her hips and breasts gently swelling; even the curve of her back is womanly. Her face, though darker than she would like, is the face of a dreaming madonna, a placid oval with wide cheekbones and skin smooth as laurel leaves. The paw-print birthmark on her cheek still makes her unhappy. Never since she was a little girl has anyone mentioned her birthmark, but she is always conscious of it, as if this mark proclaims some shameful secret.

She is too old now to cover it by letting her hair hang loose, but in moments of stress or surprise, her hand flies up to hide it. In the street she wears a shawl over her head in the country fashion, drawn up to mask her lower face. Even at home, in the patio she covers herself with a shawl.

To Luz Filomena's great regret, it has been some time since Nieves went to school. With great determination her aunt kept her at the Instituto Sor Juana Inés de la Cruz long enough to receive her primary certificate from the nuns, but she simply could not be persuaded to continue for the secondary certificate. She was never sullen or rebellious or unwilling to please her aunt Lucha, but after a while the tonic did her no good. Her headaches persisted and grew worse. Once, on the way to school she fainted in the street; old

Amparo, on her way to the market, found her not far from
the house.

"Poor little one, lying in the street like a dead dog, no
one to know what had happened to her," Amparo scolded
Luz Filomena. "God grant the next time it happens, she
won't be far away, in some street where nobody goes."

For several weeks, Nieves stayed home. She was smiling
and cheerful, helping or directing the maids. Luz Filomena
had to admit she was a great help at home. She was strong
and willing, and no household task was beyond her. When
she, instead of Amparo, went to the market, there were no
rotten tangerines among the fruit, the lettuce was fresh and
unwilted, the eggs were not broken, and more money was
left in the household purse at the end of the week.

When she seemed to have recovered, Luz Filomena sent
her back to school, but the very first day when she stood
up to recite, she fainted dead away. The Mother Superior
sent for Luz Filomena, and with many head shakings and
expressions of regret on both sides, Nieves was taken home
once more.

She felt she could be so happy just staying there, sweeping
the patio or helping with the washing in the deep stone tubs
where sunlight patterned the water like a shimmering net.
She liked to look at the sky and the flowers in the tubs with
which Luz Filomena filled the patio. She liked the trees
and the flowering vines; one in particular, a heavenly blue
morning-glory that twined around the branches of a big
mesquite, reminded her of the one at the *ranchecito*.

"Amparo, look," she said every morning when the blossoms opened bluer than the sky. "Our tree is full of happiness today," and she herself was full of happiness.

One night after all the household has gone to bed, Nieves
hears a man's voice outside her bedroom door. "Open the

door, little one. I can't sleep. I've been thinking of you, and I must see you."

Full of dreams, not even thinking who this could be, she unlocks the door and sees her aunt's husband.

"Señor Tío," the girl begins in astonishment, but he silences her.

"Don't call me by that name," he says urgently. "I've been thinking of you in my bed. You're in my mind so I can't sleep. You've grown so beautiful."

This makes her laugh, but softly, so that she forgets to keep the door, behind which she has been standing, between them, and before she knows what is happening, he is in the room with her and relocking the door.

"Don't make any noise, be careful," he warns, pushing her gently toward the bed. While she is still wondering what to say, he forces her down on the narrow bed. In her nightgown, she can hardly rebuff his caresses. Grunting and sighing, he is upon her; his hands, his knees are everywhere. She has barely realized what is happening before he is finished.

Rolling heavily to one side, the stout, still-young man, perspiring, half-clothed, sits on the edge of Nieves' bed and takes his head in his hands. He rocks back and forth rhythmically, shaking his head, sighing and groaning; she is afraid he will wake the household after all.

"Please, don't mind, don't feel bad," she comforts him. "It's all right, Señor, you couldn't help yourself."

After a short while, he leaves her, only slightly disheveled. He presses her hand to his lips in farewell. Nieves locks her bedroom door behind him. She changes her nightgown. So this is what it means to be a woman, she thinks. With her left hand, the one the Señor kissed, she reaches up to her cheek to feel the Devil's mark. It is the same; she herself is the same and yet not the same.

From that night on, her life continues quietly as before, centered upon her aunt's house and the patio. Luz Filomena no longer tries to change her. When she asks Nieves to go with her to church or the movies, or to sit in the Plaza Mayor on a Sunday evening when the jolly little municipal band is playing, or to stroll in the Jardín when the boys and girls promenade, Nieves refuses, smiling her dreamy smile.

The Señor Tío asks her, "Wouldn't you like to come along on our next trip to the capital? You're a young lady now. You can accompany your aunt."

But she replies, "If my aunt needs me, I'll come," ducking her head so the left side of her face, where the mark is, remains in shadows.

She doesn't go. In the morning, nothing lies before her but the day itself, blue as the morning-glories twined around the old tree. The sound of her broom on the patio stones is soothing and rhythmical. The liquid song of the caged thrushes, the shrill peremptory crowing of the neighbor's rooster, even the far-off barking of the dogs in the streets are pleasing to her.

The Señor never repeats the nighttime episode. She has not expected him again and would have been confused and upset if his behavior toward her had changed in any way. Whenever he speaks to her, though, her hand flies to cover her cheek. Nieves is not even aware of the gesture, which has become characteristic of her.

8

DURING THE YEARS that made a young woman of the child Nieves, with her monkeylike gestures and sudden smile, Luz Filomena has changed little. She is plumper but as lively and busy as before, and any secret anxieties are concealed by a face as smooth as ever. She dresses in the latest styles, from her sunglasses rimmed with gold wire to the cork-soled sandals on her shapely feet, and when she sometimes wears a rebozo, it is from an expensive shop near the tourist hotels.

She has made friends with several of the artists who do designing for the factory, and one of her cronies is Blanche Tole, an energetic North American woman of an indeterminate age. Her friend keeps Luz Filomena in touch with the world, with the political and artistic capitals, but the rush of events can be very deceptive. Sometimes, caught in the press of history, she feels that because something is happening elsewhere, everything must be changing, and life itself can no longer be the same. But although history has killed many and altered others out of all recognition, the quality of life has not changed. The revolutions have not much altered the life of the country people; the plowing, the planting, and the harvest wrenched from the uplands go on as before, and in the town the daily struggle is not noticeably affected by far-off war and peace or footsteps on the moon. Old Amparo now takes her corn and lime to be ground at the neighborhood mill instead of grinding it by hand at home, and she flattens her tortillas in a wooden press instead of patting them between her palms, but she has only exchanged one set of duties for another, for the tortillas must still be made to feed the family. And each life must be lived according to its secret destiny. Is it still possible for Luz Filomena to have a child?

When the Señor is away, she sometimes sits late over a bottle of yellow tequila with her friend Blanche, whom she calls Bianca, taking turns pouring the drinks into tiny clay cups that hold only a few tablespoonfuls. On Blanche's starry terrace or in the patio on the Street of the Arches, they talk about happenings inside and outside the town, especially the civil rights movement, in which Blanche is passionately involved at her home in the United States. Twice married and twice divorced, she cherishes a real bitterness toward men, blaming them for what she considers the waste of her life.

"The first time I was married, I was only a kid," she tells Luz Filomena in her hoarse, faintly accented voice, pushing back a lock of hair with a tanned hand. "I didn't know it was possible to do anything else. I'd been brought up that way, and so had all my girlfriends. Only one or two of them weren't pregnant by the time they got married. I was, myself, with Jimmy. We thought we knew a lot more than our mothers did because we knew about rubbers and diaphragms, but, my God, were we ignorant." After a pause to light a cigarette, she continues with a laugh, "And so they were married and lived happily ever after. Except we didn't. The boy was a jerk, and he had a grievance against me and Jimmy: we'd tricked him, you see. *He* hadn't wanted a wife and baby! God, how we hated each other! Finally I got enough money from my parents for a divorce."

The unaccustomed words hang in the air between them. Never before has Luz Filomena known anyone to talk so openly, but she recognizes that this is the new freedom.

"So there I was, nineteen years old with a kid and no husband. That was my big chance, right? My second chance.

I was going to art school. My mother took care of Jimmy while I was in class, but I muffed it again. I had to show someone – who knows who: my dad? my mother? – that I could still get a man."

She laughs with a cackle more than a laugh. "Ten years later, there I was again, back on Mom's neck, only by that time there were four of us. Lee and Sita were in nursery school, and Archie, my second husband, was busy having what he called a nervous breakdown. Now the kids are all grown up, I'm free to do what I should've been doing all along. And, thank God, Lee and Sita don't have the same hang-ups I had."

Luz Filomena admires Blanche very much, especially her independence. Blanche's daughters, big blond girls with their mother's open friendliness but without her energy, have both visited the town. Lee, the older, works for a television network in New York, and Sita is teaching in a rural school in Mississippi. The son, Jimmy, whom Luz Filomena has not met, is a doctor.

"You ought to get out of here, Lucy," Blanche says. "That husband of yours doesn't appreciate you. It's not too late. This is no kind of a life for you. You need an atmosphere with scope."

But although she enjoys these evenings with her friend, Luz Filomena knows that her life will not change. Unlike Blanche, she knew what to expect when she married the Señor Tío, and she has got more or less what she bargained for. She says, "Next year I think I am going to travel again, to Europe this time."

"Goddamn, you know that isn't what I mean," says Blanche affectionately. She pushes back her hair and crosses her trousered legs. It seems dreadful to her that Luz Filomena does not want to change.

"It's a goddamn shame, a woman like you," she says.
"Ay, Bianca," Luz Filomena says ruefully. The two
women smile at each other. They are good friends.

Now that Nieves is grown up, she and her aunt are friends
too, although their relationship has altered since Nieves
stopped going to school. She has slipped gradually into overseeing and helping the maids with the chores, and Luz Filomena has come to accept her in that role. When Blanche began designing for the factory, shortly after she first came to
the town, she planned a big party. Before she realized what
she was doing, Luz Filomena had offered Nieves' services.

"You will find her willing, a hard worker, and very
strong," Luz Filomena promised. "And she knows how
Americans like things done. She cooks — I taught her myself — and she has prepared parties at my house." When
Blanche asked what would be appropriate pay for Nieves
for an afternoon and evening's work, Luz Filomena was
taken aback. "Why, there's no need to pay her. She's my
niece. She'll be glad to do it." Blanche gave Nieves thirty
pesos anyway.

Since then, Nieves has been in demand among friends of
Blanche and then among their friends, because she is a hard
worker and a good cook, clever at arranging salads and
fruits. She stays cheerfully to clean up afterward and seldom
breaks anything. She stores her payment of thirty pesos or
so at the bottom of her wardrobe, where as a girl she kept
the trinkets her aunt gave her. Naturally, Luz Filomena
never pays her anything, for she helps in the house as a
member of the family. But as Amparo grows more feeble,
although neither she nor her aunt notices, Nieves is doing
more and more of the household work.

9

IT WAS NOT for some months after the Señor Tío had invaded her room that Nieves knew she was pregnant. It hardly seemed possible to her that so short an act should be made flesh with such long-lasting consequences. At the same time, she believed that every act of intercourse resulted in conception. And so she was trapped between her own vague sensations, the changes in her body, and the superstitious ideas picked up from the giggling girls at school and overheard in the talk of the women. Two months went by before she asked old Amparo for advice.

She waited until evening and then brewed some manzanilla tea for herself and Amparo. When the tea was ready, she put two cups, a sugar bowl, and a plate of sweet cakes on a tray, which she carried to Amparo's room. Nieves sat on the bed and Amparo in her wicker chair that whispered whenever she moved, and, sipping the clear, hot tea, the girl told her old friend what was bothering her.

"Do you know of a cure that will bring on the bleeding?" she asked timidly.

"Ay, Nieves!" sighed the old woman. "What are you telling me? My poor child, if what you say is true, time is the only cure for your condition."

"But surely the women know of something," Nieves insisted quietly.

Amparo laughed. "Too late for all that, my dear, too late now. I wouldn't want to promise you the impossible. There are teas you can make from *ocotillo* or *ortiguilla* or even rosemary, but never have I known of a case where drinking them prevented a baby."

"But how can you be so sure?" persisted Nieves. Amparo laughed again; it sounded like the triumphant cackle of a hen. "Drink your teas, my dear. They won't hurt you, but it will take at least six months more to cure your trouble." Sighing deeply, she stood up with difficulty and put her arms around the girl. "It's not so bad," she said. "This has happened to women before you."

Leaving Amparo's room, Nieves felt a secret twinge of satisfaction. She had tried to escape her predicament, but there was a certain relief in learning that she could do nothing but submit to her destiny.

She was glad that Amparo had not asked about the child's father, for she could never reveal him. Even the Señor Tío need not know. She would not let a shadow fall on her aunt's contentment. Let her think it was one of the poor helpless drunkards who stumbled against the big wooden doors and were admitted to sleep in the patio. Nevertheless, in another few months Luz Filomena could not help noticing what was happening.

"Nieves, my poor little one, why didn't you tell me earlier? How much you must have suffered," she mourned, embracing her niece. Later, to her American friend, she said, "So young, to have her life ruined."

"How ruined?" Blanche asked. "Do you mean it will spoil her chances of marriage?"

"I don't suppose it would do that," Luz Filomena said.

"And I don't suppose you intend to force her to leave your house."

"To leave my house? Certainly not! I feel totally responsible for her, now more than ever, even if she weren't my sister's child."

"And you aren't going to make her give up the baby."

"Of course not! What an idea! Is that what you would do in the United States?"

"All too likely," Blanche said, "or else, these days, if she could afford it, she'd probably have an abortion."

The two women contemplated the idea from opposite sides of a gulf that had suddenly widened between them. They had always known the differences between them were as profound as their agreements, but this was the first time they had been confronted with one without warning.

"I really admire the way you people feel about these things," Blanche said slowly. "You don't talk about blame. The child isn't stigmatized."

"Not until he goes to school, but from then on, whenever he has to show his documents – "

"I didn't know about that, but I meant at home," Blanche went on. "It seems, to an outsider at least, that you're just as happy over an illegitimate baby and that a poor family is as happy as a wealthy one."

"We do like babies."

"And yet it would be better for Mexico if the birth rate went down, better for the babies already born."

"These things are not for us to decide."

"And yet you said your niece's life is ruined."

Meanwhile Nieves continued to do her work in the house. Her mother heard the news and came every month to make sure that the fetus was in the correct position. She urged Nieves to use the traditional methods to ensure a well-formed infant, but Nieves said, smiling, "The doctor told me you don't need to tie a key on your stomach if you are healthy."

She felt unusually well. Nothing tired her, and nothing could ruffle her deepening lazy calm. She felt she could be happy all her days if she could stay just as she was now, and yet she knew her contentment came from the anticipation of cradling her baby in her arms.

Although Luz Filomena had commiserated with her, she did not try to take Nieves with her to the Virgin of Dolores when she lit candles for the baby's safe delivery, and never had she asked her for the father's name. That question hardly occurred to her. It clearly did not trouble Nieves. Despite her disappointment over Nieves' future, she felt an undeniable pleasure at the idea of having a baby in the house. It would make up for the barren years of her own life, in a way Nieves' presence alone could not.

10

THE SHORT UPLAND WINTER was over, and a faint powdering of green was everywhere, on the gently swelling ocean of the plains, along the roadsides, and on the stiff tree branches, still awkward in their wintry postures, when Nieves' child was born. She calmly watched the hurried preparations of her aunt and Amparo. One of the young maids ran for the doctor, another for the midwife. Lights flashed on everywhere, setting wild shadows dancing in the patio. The Señor Tío was out of town, or he would probably have taken Nieves to the hospital; she herself much preferred to remain at home.

The midwife, toothless and cheerful, older even than Amparo, arrived ahead of the doctor and, after a single glance into the room where Nieves was lying, emptied her bag onto the kitchen table. Water was already boiling in two large pots. She asked that some cooking oil also be heated, and she made a tea by adding to one of the pots some mint leaves, cinnamon bark, and wood chips from a guazuma tree. When the oil was hot, she carried it in to Nieves and began to massage her with it. Luz Filomena followed with the tea, which Nieves obediently drank. Except for the contractions, now occurring about every three minutes, she had no particular discomfort, and she smiled and talked with Amparo and her aunt.

After seeing that Nieves drank the tea, the midwife asked Amparo to prepare a drink of garlic and wild honey for Nieves after the baby was delivered, to speed the expulsion of the afterbirth.

"Will it be so soon, then?" Amparo whispered.

"Soon, soon, a few little minutes. She is young and healthy — soon, you'll see."

And before Amparo had returned with the medicine, she heard the thin wail of the newborn.

"A girl — and beautiful," the midwife cried in her high, cracked voice.

Hurrying into the bedroom, Amparo embraced Nieves and then Luz Filomena. Tears started to her eyes.

"Don't cry, little grandmother," sobbed Luz Filomena. "It's all over, and that drunken fool of a doctor hasn't come yet!"

"Ay, Lucha, I'm crying for what's beginning," Amparo said, dabbing at her eyes as she went over to the bed, where the baby lay fat and drowsy, already washed, with the cord tied and seared. "Another girl, a beautiful girl."

Nieves smiled sleepily. Even before they left her alone with the child, she had fallen into a doze. She did not hear the doctor bustling in.

"I hope you don't expect to be paid," Luz Filomena told him. "Half an hour ago was when we needed you, not now."

Sheepishly, the doctor stammered excuses and congratulations.

"Better this way," Amparo said, arms akimbo, as they watched him leave. "Babies are women's business."

Indeed, Nieves seldom thought of any man in connection with her child. During the eight days after the birth, when Amparo would not permit her to leave her room, she lay for hours in a stupor, admiring her daughter. She nursed her whenever she cried and bathed her daily in water scented with sweet marigold leaves. Her baby was occupation and justification for her entire existence, which now lay behind her all unknowingly directed toward this single goal. Watching the baby sleeping, she forgot the Devil's mark on her cheek. But at the birth, after counting the infant's fingers and toes, she had examined her minutely to make sure the child was unmarked.

Shortly after the return of the Señor Tío, she agreed to have the baby baptized. She had decided to call her Trinidad.

Her parents and all her brothers and sisters came in the jolting old truck; they all wore new clothes, gifts from Luz Filomena and the Señor Tío, and the infant, in a long elaborate christening gown, mewling and screwing up its red face against the sunlight, was carried on an embroidered pillow to the Church of the Virgin of Dolores. Afterward, in the flowery patio, there was a party with cold drinks for the adults and hot chocolate for the children. By this time, spring was well advanced, and blossoms were bursting out on every vine and shrub, the bougainvillaea in all its shades of magenta, pink, scarlet, and vermilion, the trumpet vine in its clear orange, the pale yellow mimosa, and the blue-violet jacaranda. The fruit trees were already leafing out, along with roses, geraniums, hibiscus, gardenias, and azaleas. Holding her infant in her arms, Nieves felt she had found her place in the world, and the world was beautiful and welcoming.

Part III

1

AS THE BIG PLANE settles with a slight tremor on the hard-baked runway at Mexico City, the passengers collect their belongings, reassembling their lives suspended during the long flight. Blinking in the brightness, they stumble toward Immigration. As one of the few Mexicans on the plane, Luz Filomena is shunted off from the tourists toward a uniformed man with his eyes invisible behind dark glasses. He scrutinizes her papers laboriously, like a child learning to read. She smiles broadly as she takes some hundred-peso notes from her handbag.

"*Pase.*" The unsmiling official motions her on, the money crumpled in his hand. "*Pase.*"

She hurries to the porter waiting with her luggage at the customs table. Already her eyes smart from the smog. She has been away from Mexico for nearly a year, and as always when she returns, she is in a turmoil of impressions. Everything assails her violently. Everything is at the same time picturesque and overwhelmingly familiar: the smooth face of the customs official, the acrid odor of tortillas, the beggars crumpled at the taxi rank with their hands outstretched and their whining "*Por caridad.*" On the long taxi ride from the airport into the city, she notices a new housing complex here, a modern office building there, the glass and steel towers of a hotel still uncompleted. The predominant impression is of the same shoddy landscape on the fringes of the city, the flat houses sinking as the underground lake drains relentlessly away. A blanket of fetid air hangs between the city and the sun, and beneath it on the gray pavements, rich and poor alike go about their daily business.

The ancient buses wheeze out black exhaust. The little curb-side stands glow with their mounds of oranges and their braziers smelling of garlic and frying oil, and when the taxi stops for a traffic light, there is the inevitable ragged boy hawking dishpans in turquoise plastic or reproductions of the Last Supper in imitation marble.

She goes directly to the bus depot of the Corceles de la Meseta. Tired of traveling, Luz Filomena is nevertheless determined to continue home as quickly as possible. The depot is crowded, noisy, and filled with every kind of traveler, from elegant ladies like herself to shapeless country grand-mothers and old men whose cracked dusty feet with broken toenails look unaccustomed to their stiff sandals. At the ticket grille her dimples and her well-filled purse gain her a window seat on the shady side of the bus.

Once they are on their way, lurching and swaying through the traffic on Insurgentes Sur out onto the Autopista, she can relax once more into the traveler's anonymity, seeing with equal indifference the monotonous countryside or the reflection of her own face in the window.

It has been a long journey from New York to Chicago to Dallas and now toward the town. During the past fifteen years the Señor Tío's serape factory has prospered, and a large plant, larger than the original, has been built in Mon-terrey, with branch offices in three cities in the United States. Luz Filomena is her husband's representative in these offices for orders, distribution, and advertising. These days, she is more out of Mexico than in it. She has sent a wire to the house on the Street of the Arches, telling Nieves when to ex-pect her, and she is hoping that it has arrived, for communi-cations remain erratic out in the country. She must compose herself for the meetings and greetings ahead, the changes and the samenesses after a year's absence.

The sun is setting as the silvery bus winds through the narrow streets of the town, and she collects her hand luggage again. The bus stops outside San Policarpo, and Luz Filomena straightens the jacket of her suit and adjusts her little mink neckpiece. She would like to slip into San Policarpo for a minute, but a boy is already carrying her luggage to a taxi, for the last leg of her trip. The taxi jolts over the cobbles, past the feebly glowing lanterns over carved wooden doors, the ancient decaying stones or crumbling plaster of the walls, and the windows heavily shuttered behind iron grilles. On a street corner she sees a knee-high pile of garbage, lumps of damp bread, vegetable peelings, animal bones with shreds of meat still clinging to them, all mixed with waxed-paper milk containers and scraps of plastic. An emaciated bitch crouches in the shadows. Luz Filomena grimaces. More than a year ago, she arranged with the municipal authorities for refuse to be collected in a truck and not dumped in the street. It will have to be arranged all over again. A man is urinating against the house wall. Caught briefly in the taxi headlights, he grins sheepishly and turns away, doing up his trousers. She draws a sharp breath of exasperation, and her fingers drum on the leather handbag in her lap. So much to be done.

At home, she pulls the leather latchstring, and the massive door swings open. Light spills into the dark street, and the patio is filled with light and the shadows of flowers, with welcoming voices and hurrying footsteps. She pays the taxi driver, and he backs out onto the cobbles, stuffing the money into his pocket without counting it. Someone has closed the wooden doors. Someone else is carrying her suitcases into a room off the patio. Out of the shadows by the stone washtubs, a woman rushes, wiping her hands on a cotton apron.

"Nieves, it's you!"

They embrace and then look at each other. All of Nieves' admiration and affection for her aunt glows in her soft eyes. Luz Filomena sees a stout woman shapeless in an apron and shawl. Her face is unlined, her smile as warm as ever, her shining dark hair pulled back into a thick braid. "Children, your aunt Lucha is here."

The shy, smiling children step up to be embraced. Trini is already seventeen, smooth and plump, soft-eyed like her mother. Remedios is sulky. Felicidad, a skinny nine-year-old, is carrying something.

"What's this?"

It is Nieves' youngest, Gabriel, fat and sleepy, an infant when Luz Filomena went away.

"Beautiful as an angel!"

Taking the heavy baby from Felicidad, Nieves settles him on her ample hip under her rebozo. His eyelids, lifted for a moment, fall once more, his long eyelashes brushing his cheek. He is asleep, nuzzling into his mother's breast.

"Ay, Nieves." Luz Filomena hardly knows her own feelings. This is homecoming. This is her world, persisting here through all the months of her absence. While she talked and laughed, was happy or lonely, went about her business in the North American cities, here Nieves, still unmarried, grew stouter, the patio was swept every morning, vegetables were brought home from the market, and the garbage was thrown into the street, where the pigs and dogs rooted.

She is half-pulled, half-pushed into the living room, where every light is blazing. There in the place of honor, under an embroidered cloth, is the new color television set.

"The Señor Tío didn't come with you?"

"He'll come in a day or two. He had to stay in Monterrey." These days, he spends most of his time at the new plant in Monterrey. Now the old factory here is maintained chiefly as an office and an attraction for tourists, who admire the huge wooden manual looms.

Trini offers her great-aunt a drink from a tray. Luz Filomena sips it politely.

"You make me feel like a guest, Trinidad."

"That won't last long," Nieves says in her soft voice, with a glance at Gabriel. She folds the child more securely in her shawl. "You have come home. Your room is all ready. Trini and Remedios have been cleaning ever since we got your telegram."

"I've come home, it's true," says Luz Filomena. But is this her home, she wonders, this world that has not changed in any meaningful way since she was a girl, where life is scratched with a wooden plow from the earth of the high plains, where beggars station themselves along the stony streets like images in some profane Calvary, where her own niece brings forth her fatherless children as thoughtlessly as a cow – this world that in spite of its television sets and fashionable clothes has never dreamed of what is thought and said and done in the cities from which she has returned. Is this her home?

"In the morning you will show me everything, tell me all that happened while I was away," she says.

2

LUZ FILOMENA IS AWAKENED by the crowing of roosters and the sound of sweeping, Mexico's most characteristic sound. From the earth-floored patios and rutted tracks of the tiniest settlement to the pavements of the capital itself, the faint, rhythmically persistent sound of sweeping welcomes the morning, until the very dust in the streets bears the mark of the indefatigable broom.

She sighs, and smiles, and gets up. So much to be done and so little hope of accomplishing it. The day before yesterday, she had an appointment with the Water Commissioner – no reason why the water supply should not be constant after construction of the new underground reservoirs – and the day before that, with the Deputy Director of Electricity. On the morning of her first day in the town, she had interviewed the Deputy of Municipal Sanitation. These men responded gallantly to her dimples and listened sympathetically to her grievances. Everything must be put in writing, they said. Yes, she had brought her written complaints, suggestions, and requests. The officials scrutinized them. This is excellent, very good, but it would be better still if these documents were notarized, not that anyone would doubt her word or their authenticity, not here, but the officials in the state capital haven't the honor of knowing her or her respected family.

So she had spent another morning at the office of the notary lawyer, mostly waiting for him to see her. She arrived promptly at ten o'clock. The ancient battered doors leading into the patio were open, and nobody was sitting on the wooden bench worn smooth with years of patient waiting outside his office door. Pausing at the stone threshold, she looked down into the dimness as into a well. Faint specks of dust swam in a translucent diagonal bar of light. On the dim paneled wall, above glass-fronted bookcases stuffed with law journals in leather bindings, hung an antique mahogany clock, its pendulum motionless, its emaciated hands of gilt filigree stopped at a quarter to five. Next to it were several diplomas and certificates, flyspecked and barely visible behind glass, and a gas lamp on a bracket in case of electrical failure. Off to the left, a dark flight of steps rose into further darkness. Below, on the cool stone floor three desks were wedged together in the center of the little room, all of them crowded with stacks of books, dust-covered documents, and limp manila folders, some closed, some open. In the midst of the clutter were three telephones whose snaky black wires gave the effect of crawling in and out among the legal affairs, and on one desk an electric typewriter was tapping briskly under the hands of a bored young man who did not look up from the document he was copying. Behind the desk facing Luz Filomena, an old man was dozing. His head was thrust forward tortoiselike, and his sparse hair was extraordinarily white. In that aqueous gloom his papery skin had a greenish cast. The pale rubbery lips were clamped on an unlighted cigar. Every minute or so, his head would jerk downward and then, possibly by some dream-inspired effort of the will, would gradually rise again. Once from a frosted-glass door under the stairs, a miniskirted secretary darted out briefly, saying "Excuse me!" to nobody in particular. Otherwise nothing intruded on the shaft of light, the staccato tapping of the typewriter, and the periodic head jerking of the old man.

She cleared her throat. The typist lifted his eyes and nodded at her. She took the documents from her handbag and began to explain that she had been advised to see the lawyer, but he nodded again, motioned her to the bench outside the office door, and resumed his typing.

When she was in Monterrey or the States, life back at home seemed a dream, as if it could not go on the same way the whole time she was gone and then continue after her return, as if nothing were happening anywhere, as if everything were not continually changing everywhere else. But each time she came back, she found the same cracks in the chimney where the workmen had not used enough water in the cement, the same leaky roof over the washtubs, Nieves or one of her children sweeping with the same broken broom. The coexistence of these two modes gave her an uneasy sensation like seasickness or the sudden fear when a car's gears slip.

When she'd mentioned this concern to her North American friend, Blanche Tole had laughed and remarked, "Isn't that what gives all this its charm? It's never-never land. It's not real life. People come here to get away from real life."

Luz Filomena was not satisfied. It was real enough for her people: for Julia and Fausto, grown drier and more silent every year as the thirsty land sucked their lives away, for old Amparo, a huddle of rags out of which still peered her wise eyes like dark windows in a ruined house, for the beggars around every street corner like eroded statues of reproach, for gentle and stubborn Nieves, whose life she had intended to be different but whose four children were real enough. And yet she understood her friend from the frenetic world of international politics with morning coffee, economic catastrophe for lunch, and ecological disaster at dinnertime.

Blanche, looking up ruefully into Luz Filomena's eyes, had added quickly, "No, Lucha, suffering is real everywhere. You can't limit it geographically. I don't forget it. Someone wrote that everything is repeated in Mexico, even the blood sacrifices of the Aztecs. Myself, I feel that everything is repeated, at every moment, all over the world. Nothing can be put in the past tense."

Now Luz Filomena sat on the wooden bench between an old man from the country and a nervous North American woman, her head a mass of calculatedly tousled gray curls, her feet strapped into the sturdy sandals that guidebooks recommend for walking on cobbled streets. Her husband stood glancing alternately at his watch and at some papers, as if he expected that at the stroke of some predetermined hour the papers would disappear. Nobody spoke.

Everything was repeated endlessly, she thought. Not only was there much that needed to be done, but everything needed to be done over and over. Accomplishing something was not like climbing a tree or a pyramid but like walking in a circle, passing the same point again and again as the earth retraces its orbit around the sun.

This morning, remembering that interminable wait as she brushes her hair and twists it up from the nape of her neck, she sighs and smiles again. She had eventually been admitted to the upstairs room, where the lawyer had briskly notarized her documents, pocketed his fee, and shown her to the door more gallantly than even the government officials.

So much to be done. She has still to meet with the women who are setting up a free clinic for infants at the hospital and with another group forming a society for the protection of animals. Blanche Tole has said something about establishing free meals for schoolchildren. Today, however, she and Remedios, Nieves' second daughter, are driving out into the country to visit Julia. She invited Trinidad and Nieves, but Trini has errands to do with a friend, and these days

Nieves is more reluctant than ever to leave the house. She is her own prisoner, locked behind the massive carved doors. She seldom goes even to the market or to church or to the little dark doorway where they grind the corn. There is always some reason to stay home: the truck might come with the gas, or she must watch a stew so it won't burn, or little Gabriel is teething or last night had a touch of the colic.

3

REMEDIOS, A DARK SULLEN GIRL of fourteen who inherited from her unknown father the features of a fashion model, had not been eager to visit her grandparents, but she finally agreed almost perversely. Such a silent, sulky girl is not much company, and Luz Filomena would prefer the smiling Trinidad. But the day is bright, and although the farm depresses her, she is looking forward to seeing her sister.

Remedios brings two cups of coffee and sets one for Luz Filomena on the glass-topped dressing table. Sipping the other, she watches her aunt put up her hair and examine her face in the mirror.

"Aunt Lucha, Mamá wants us to bring back some honey if there is any."

Luz Filomena smiles at her. "How I loved that country honey when I was your age."

Remedios says nothing. They walk out through the patio to the car, a gleaming anachronism in the dusty street.

Luz Filomena is a good driver, and after the town's steep and bumpy streets, the road is straight and smooth. They travel fast, and Remedios begins to hum.

"You like the country?" Luz Filomena asks, feeling her way with this difficult, dour child.

"It's all right. It's pretty, I suppose," Remedios says. "It's better than that town."

"You don't like the town? People come from all over the world to visit it. They admire it."

"I hate it. It's like being buried alive. What difference does a beautiful tombstone make to the corpse?"

Now Luz Filomena recognizes the source of the girl's sul-

lenness, her silence and hostility. As a girl, behind her mask
of smiles and dimples, she had felt the same, waking to the
tedium of the plains, waiting for the school bus and watching life speed by in a fast car on the very highway they are
traveling now.

"Are you going to school? Do you like to study?" she
asks.

"I don't know. Most of the time I go, unless Mamá or
Trini needs me at home." The sullen mask is back in place.

They are close to the familiar turnoff to the farm. The
road, widened and improved, is still a dirt road but no
longer the rutted overgrown track across the scrubby fields.

"I don't even have a father," Remedios says. "I can't ever
amount to anything."

"Nonsense," her aunt snaps. "If you don't amount to anything, you'll have only yourself to blame – not your father,
not your mother. But if you really want to get out of the
town – "

"I do."

"I'll help you. But first you must go to school."

They both sigh, but Luz Filomena's sigh is more profound,
because her banal requirement risks losing the girl just as
she's almost won her over.

"That's what the sisters say – and the teachers at the Secondary," Remedios says dully.

"It's true."

They stop at the low wall around the farmhouse, and
here is Julia in her countrywoman's apron and shawl, hurrying out of the doorway, low and dark as the entrance to a
cave. At first glance, the grandmother Julia and her daughter Nieves might be taken for sisters; they share that ageless
quality of the plains and mountains.

"Lucha! After such a long time!" The sisters embrace,

their cheeks wet with tears. A closer look at Julia reveals
the face of a mummy, darkened by the sun and crisscrossed
with wrinkles, her mouth sunken where teeth have fallen
out, her black hair thinning. Her hands are hard and curled
like claws. "Times are hard, but we are still here."

"I heard in the town some talk of flooding you out and
building another dam," Luz Filomena says, when they are
sitting under the flowering vines in the patio.

"Talk, nothing but talk," says Julia. "They are making a
new dam. Who knows when it will be finished, with the
government the way it is. But it's over on the other side of
the highway. We never took that talk seriously. But there
was other talk, that people from the north wanted to buy
all this land and divide it into lots and build houses for people from the city."

"Would you and Fausto have to sell?"

"If everyone else sells, what could we do? But right now
it's come to nothing. You've seen, below the town on the
other side, where they've put up their electric wires and laid
out their streets, out there in the desert, even though no one
is buying."

"It's progress."

Julia shakes her head. "I'll put up some tea." Remedios
follows her into the house.

Luz Filomena, too, shakes her head. It is progress, both
the dams to irrigate the plain and the subdivisions to popu-
late it, but progress toward what? Is there any point in ask-
ing? For thirty-seven years, Fausto and Julia, like her parents before them, have farmed this land, following the government's agricultural bulletins. Never has the earth yielded
more than the barest living, and it has sucked them dry,
body and mind. If reservoirs and roads and electric power
plants and machines and fertilizers can make people's lives

better and easier, who can say the price is too high?

Julia and Remedios return with the tea, and Julia asks after Nieves and her children. "Gabriel must be big now. I haven't seen him for months."

"Big, yes," says Luz Filomena, "a big boy, two years old, and that daughter of yours is still nursing him! It's shameful, and I told her so."

"It's the way of the country people," Julia says. "Women think as long as they nurse, they won't get more babies."

"What nonsense! Nieves knows by now what to do if she doesn't want more babies." The sisters laugh softly, like schoolgirls.

Remedios, scowling into her empty cup, feels a pang in her side, on her mother's behalf; for a moment she hates her great-aunt and grandmother. In the morning she despised her mother for being no more than an animal, for bringing her into the world a bastard, for being so placid, unruffled, and composed. And now, with the sour aftertaste of the tea rising in her throat like rage, she wants to protect her mother, who, whatever else she has done, has never laughed at anyone in that cruel, superior way.

Fausto comes in from plowing the fields all morning with Rosario, and they all go into the house for the midday meal. Afterward, as they are about to leave, Remedios remembers her mother's request and whispers to Luz Filomena.

"I almost forgot," Luz Filomena says. "Nieves asked me to bring back some honey if there is any."

"The first of the season, sister," Julia says with a smile. "Ay, Lucha, everything is changing, but the bees still make honey in the same old way."

4

ONE EVENING ON IMPULSE, Luz Filomena takes Trinidad with her to visit Blanche Tole. She has been thinking of introducing the dark, discontented Remedios to Blanche; those two would understand each other, and perhaps the American woman could help the girl. But Trini crosses the patio just as Luz Filomena is about to walk down to light a candle at the Virgin of Dolores in the last rosy light that, unlike the dim twilights of the north, gives everything an almost painful clarity before being blotted out by the abrupt nightfall.

"How would you like to walk down to the church with me?"

Trini agrees to go. She is the most docile and placid of Nieves' children, at seventeen already plump and soft, content to spend her days helping her mother take care of the Señor Tío's house and her evenings, when the electricity does not fail, watching the television programs from Mexico City. Her best friend, Teresa, has been working in the rug factory at good pay for almost a year, but Trini stays home, although the hours at the factory are no longer than the hours of sweeping and scrubbing in the house without any wages. Teresa has coaxed her to take a job, but Trini only laughs and says, "Maybe someday, maybe tomorrow."

Now Luz Filomena asks her, "And how is it that such a pretty girl is free to come out with an old aunt in the evening? Where's your *boyfriend*?" She uses the English word.

Trini laughs. "I have no boyfriend, Aunt Lucha."

"A girl like you — all the boys look at you when you pass by. I've seen them," persists Luz Filomena. "You must have a sweetheart."

Still smiling, Trini says, "I've seen what happens to my friends and their sweethearts, Aunt Lucha. My mother, even. I have enough babies already to take care of. I don't want any more. I don't want a sweetheart, not for a long time. Maybe when I'm thirty, I'll get married, or maybe I won't get married at all."

"What do you want to do – have a job, a profession?"

"Oh, I couldn't do that."

"If you went back to school, got your certificate – "

Trini laughs. "I don't think school is for me. While I was there, the sisters tried to teach me, but it was no use."

"What does your mother say?"

"My mother doesn't talk about it. She doesn't take much interest in us big ones, anyway. It's the babies she cares about, especially Gabriel."

Luz Filomena feels the old guilt, like a twinge of rheumatism in rainy weather, whenever she comes home and finds Nieves nursing another baby, apparently content to be an unpaid servant. This life is not what she had intended when she took Nieves from her mother in the country. And now she is confronted by this second amiable girl, stubborn beneath her smiling docility.

It is when they leave the church that Luz Filomena thinks of visiting Blanche Tole. Trini, as always, is agreeable. The two women thread their way through the steep streets fitfully lit by the wrought-iron lamps above the carved doors.

"Lucy, I was just thinking about you," the North American woman exclaims, drawing them inside.

Trini does not speak English, so the conversation begins in Spanish. Blanche has been staying in this borrowed house for a month, and next week she will return to the United States.

"I can't stay here too long any more," she explains, switch-

ing to English. "I'm just not cut out to be an expatriate. It
makes me uncomfortable to be recognized as an American.
I'll never forget when I first came down here, when I started
doing designs for your husband, Lucy. My landlord said to
me, 'Why do you keep exploding these hydrogen bombs?
Why don't you listen to what the world says? The whole
world says you must stop testing those bombs!' I was taken
aback that he thought I would approve of a thing like that.
'*I* don't test the bombs,' I said. 'I think the bombs are terrible. I march in demonstrations carrying a sign that says
STOP NUCLEAR TESTING.' But he didn't even hear me. He
just kept repeating, 'Why do you do it?'" She pauses to
drink some of her beer, looking to see if their glasses need
refilling. "Now I think the old man was right. I was responsible for those bomb tests in spite of my parades and signs,
just as I was responsible for burning Vietnamese with na-
palm and bombing civilians. I'm responsible for Cambodia.
I'm responsible for what my country does in Central America. I'm an American, and I'm responsible, not that there's
a damned thing I can do about it! And now with this struggle on our hands – "

Trini asks, "What is the struggle now?"

Blanche laughs shortly. "Women! The liberation of
women. My God, that's the trouble. When I'm down here,
I can hardly believe it exists as a serious movement."

*A woman doing her washing in the stream, carrying a
heavy basket home from the market with a baby already in
her shawl, one or two little ones clutching at her skirts and
another on the way, a woman cooking in a windowless
room with a dirt floor, all afternoon scouring the pots in
cold water with a handful of straw – her sisters, her spokes-
women, demanding the freedom to live like a man.*

"Sometimes, here, the social planners' arguments seem

as relevant to the lives of real people – especially, my God, real women – as the arguments about how many angels could stand on the head of a pin. And how many real people there are, not only here, all over the world."

Struggling to pull themselves out of the swamp of preindustrial superstition and into the horrors and rewards of industrialization, while the other half of the world has already begun to bewail the lost innocence of illiteracy, unrefined flour, and the alternation of feast and famine in an agricultural society.

"Women! So they crawled out of the doll's house built for them by one generation, were taught how to use machines and were employed by another, told by a third that by doing this they had denied their true nature and doomed themselves thereby, and now they're being accused of conniving at their own enslavement and trading their birthright for a mess of pottage."

Lucha, relaxed in a wood and leather chair, nods and smiles. For her it has been a personal struggle to get here, to this house, being friends with this woman. She has escaped from the planting and harvesting and from the stone washtubs. She is like the "self-made man" who thinks that what he accomplished with such difficulty ought not to be made easy. Wasn't the struggle essential to the triumph of success? Sometimes she believes that the struggle itself is the triumph. Is her so-called success any more significant than Julia's or Nieves' ways of living?

And what does Trinidad make of it all? She sits there sipping her Coca-Cola. Ever since she was small, she has known her aunt Lucha's friend Bianca, with her sweeping gestures and untidy hair streaked with gray. Her hoarse voice soothes her. Every now and then she catches a word: "women...machines...slavery." She watches the restless fingers, quick and deft at sketching the pictures she admires. It does not occur to Trini that anything Bianca is saying might touch her personally. In these abstractions she does not recognize Julia, Nieves, Lucha, or herself. She enjoys the sound of the words going on and on, like listening to the priest in church or to singers on television and the records her aunt brings from the States. Her life goes on pleasantly from day to day. She is happy to accept a diversion, like going to the shops with her friend Teresa or going to the Virgin of Dolores with Luz Filomena, and otherwise she sweeps the patio, hangs up the washed clothes, and keeps an eye on her little brother. Her mother, Lucha, and the Señor Tío seem changeless to her. She does not remember them younger or think about what might happen when they and she are older. When she sings *"Miserere nobis, ora pro nobis,"* she is moved by the swelling music of the organ under the singing voices. She does not contemplate the words of the song or of the sermon: "Obedience…cchastity…diligence…woman's duty."

"Trinidad, Lucy tells me you would like to go to the United States."

Trini smiles and dimples.

5

NIEVES HAD NEVER BEEN especially interested in men and had never thought that she might attract their honorable attention. She imagined that the Devil's mark on her cheek branded her, above the roundnesses and softnesses of her body, so that every man recognized in her his legitimate prey. In any case, woman was the natural prey of man, and thus the Señor Tío's passion had not alarmed or even surprised her.

The act that transformed her from a virgin to a woman neither attracted nor repelled her. It happened only once and seemed less significant than her menstrual blood, which linked her with the warm blood of everything on earth, the dark tides in the earth's veins, and the phases of the moon.

Her pregnancy changed these rhythms, but she quickly noticed new tides of feeling in her swelling body. By the time of her delivery, all her physical sensations seemed centered in her womb, and everything else in the world seemed tangential. She transferred that primal significance to the infant, and then her own body receded in importance except as a source of nourishment for the baby. Long after Trini could walk, Nieves continued to nurse her. Amparo scolded her, but Nieves took great pleasure in pressing the heavy child to her breast inside her shawl, and she listened to no one's advice.

When Trinidad was two years old, Nieves craved another infant, tiny and helpless. She was not interested in marrying and leaving the Señor Tío's house to wait on some rough stranger who might not respect her once he saw her little girl. And she had no interest in promenading in the Jardín and giggling with other girls on the wrought-iron benches. So one night when the Señor Tío and Luz Filomena were out of town and she was awakened by a drunken thundering on the wooden doors to the patio, she slipped out in her nightgown, as the soft-hearted maids had when she was a little girl, and let him in, whoever he might be, lost on the Street of the Arches between the swinging doors of the cantinas and his own house far out in the country. But this time, instead of leaving him to sleep on a pile of sacks under the concrete steps in a corner of the patio, she led him in the darkness to her own bed. When he woke in the morning, bleary-eyed and mumbling, she had been gone long since. Nieves never spoke of the episode, and she would not recognize the man if he passed her on the street. She was pregnant again and happy. That was how Remedios was conceived.

According to the teachings of the Church, Nieves was doing wrong, but she had never been devout. At Trinidad's christening, she had seen everything with cold new eyes. The echoing stone vault of the nave was like a tomb. The silver font, with cherubs supporting the great basin, reminded her of a few silver coins in the wrinkled hand of a beggar. The life-sized plaster figures all around frightened her with their painted grimaces. There was no comfort for her and her daughter here or in the priest's sententious sonorities. What did he know of a woman's life?

She had looked down at Trinidad asleep on her embroidered pillow and felt a sudden pang — of anger? grief? remorse? — at having brought another being into this world by an almost accidental encounter. The priest's words thundered down on the child's defenseless head. From that day, Nieves had never visited the church except for the babies' christenings. The Señor Tío paid for them, and to refuse would have required explanations and arguments.

After she was finished nursing Remedios, on moonless nights Nieves silently unbarred the doorway for drunken men, but she did not become pregnant. She took no interest in the men or pleasure in the sexual act, a mere means to an end. Never was she more proud of her body than when her belly swelled under her apron. Now, as the months went by and she did not become pregnant, she withdrew further into silence. Trinidad and Remedios, three years younger, concerned her less and less, although she tried to treat them as a mother should.

Aunt Lucha made a pet of the amiable Trini when she was small, taking her everywhere, dressing her in hand-sewn expensive dresses, and buying her candy and toys. She would have done the same for Nieves' second daughter, but Remedios would turn her head away and pretend not to hear. Sometimes she had tantrums, screaming and drumming her bare heels on the patio stones until they bled. Nieves would carry her to the kitchen and cradle her, crooning, until she quieted.

Several times during these years Nieves thought she was with child, but each time something went wrong, and her tears mixed with the blood flowing out of season. She felt guilty then, as if she had murdered the unborn, as if her attempts to abort Trini had belatedly succeeded. But finally when Trinidad was twelve years old, Nieves became pregnant again, and she was less taciturn and withdrawn. She hoped for a boy, and Luz Filomena lit candles every week. When a third girl was delivered, Nieves forgot to be disappointed and named her Felicidad.

Now Nieves, who had been pretty, gently rounded, timid as a deer on her delicate legs, had broadened like a potato. Her silence, never sullen or hostile, was the silence of an animal that gives tongue only in pain or as a warning. Waking in the morning, she welcomed the new day, and lying down at night beside the baby Felicidad, she welcomed sleep. Her life lacked only one thing, a son.

When Felicidad was three years old, Gabriel was born. Never again did Nieves unbar the patio door to a drunken country fellow. Her heart was full of compassion for them, as it was for all poor creatures stumbling sore-footed over the cobbles far from home, but no longer did she admit them in secret to the darkness of the garden.

GABRIEL HAS THE plump cheeks, tiny pointed chin, and enormous velvety black eyes of a painted cherub. Wings sprouting from his sturdy shoulders would not look out of place. He is ferociously dirty. His hands and feet are caked with dried mud or gray with the dust of the street, and his face is sticky with the juice of sweet fruit or smeared with jam or honey. It is usually streaked with tears as well, because he has the temperament of a petty despot. He rules his mother with an iron hand, and any frustration of his wishes produces howls, shrieks, and torrents of tears, as if he were being beaten as hard as his sister Remedios would like him beaten. But no one lifts a finger to him. His every wish is granted, and if there is a delay, his screams inform the world of his displeasure. He likes all candy, chewing gum, and sodas, and he amuses himself also by playing with wax matches. Brick and stone do not catch fire, but he has burned holes in his shirt, and once, imitating the older boys in the street with their firecrackers, he threw a lighted match that fell on Felicidad's leg.

That was an afternoon for screaming. Felicidad's screams, although out of proportion to her actual pain, could not even approximate the vastness of her outrage. Gabriel joined in, at first in fright for hurting his sister, then in terror of punishment. He need not have worried. Hurrying from the kitchen, a cold hand clutching at her heart, Nieves caught up her son to her breast, and then, seeing Felicidad's burn, she doctored her with ointment. Still sniffling, Gabriel stood by his mother's chair and watched. Felicidad stopped crying in her mother's lap and buried her face in that warm soft

breast, but as soon as she had finished smoothing the ointment over the burn, Nieves told her to get down.

"I have my work to do. I can't sit here all morning," she
said good-naturedly, giving the child a little pat. "Go wash
your face in some cold water."

Putting his thumb in his mouth, Gabriel pulled at his
mother's skirt. "I'm hungry."

"Come on then. I'll fix a roll with jam for you, greedy
one," Nieves said with a sigh.

"I want some too," Felicidad chimed in.

Without speaking, Nieves spread a second roll with jam.

It is only in the past month or two that Gabriel has dared
to venture outside the patio into the street. Nieves does not
want him to do it; it makes her very uneasy, but she does
nothing to prevent him from leaving. At his age, the little
girls had been content to stay in the garden, except for trips
with Nieves and Lucha to the market and the square. But
Gabriel is another matter, and now he is big enough to
reach the latchstring of the wooden doors.

He does not go far, only down to the arches at the bottom
of the street, where the stream flows into the refuse-choked
tunnel and the stray dogs and pigs root in the garbage, and
to the little store, where the big boys buy candy, matches,
firecrackers, and cigarettes. She can usually tell when he is
in the street, since he is unable to pull the heavy doors shut
behind him. When she sees them gaping open, Nieves walks
down the length of the garden calling him. When he can,
the storekeeper keeps an eye on him, "my youngest client."

Sunday afternoon is always quiet on the Street of the
Arches, even when Luz Filomena is home. After the big midday meal, everyone is resting. Trini's records from the
States, turned low, form a counterpoint to the church bells
and the chirruping caged birds on the patio wall.

Nieves, lying on her bed, is jerked to her feet by ear-splitting screams. Gabriel's voice – but where is he? A minute earlier, he had been playing with his marbles on the floor. She runs out, cramming her feet into shoes and catching up her scarf. The doors to the street are open. Felicidad runs in, sobbing and breathless. Then she sees Gabriel, screaming and gasping for breath as he staggers up the street. One side of his face streams blood, down his neck onto the little shirt of blue and white stripes that she put on him in the morning. Nieves, for all her bulk, flies to him.

"What is it? What happened?"

Gasping and choking, he hugs her legs as tightly as he can. Very gently she begins to wipe the blood from his cheek with her shawl.

"Felicidad! What happened?" The sobbing little girl clutches her skirt.

"It was a dog."

Although her knees are trembling, Nieves manages to wet a cloth with cold water and wash the wound. Looking at it makes her feel faint, but she understands that Gabriel had tried to pet one of the dogs scavenging for food in the refuse pile and the dog bit clear through his cheek. To her horror, she sees Gabriel's tongue protruding through the opening.

The child's cries have subsided to sobs and hiccups when Luz Filomena, who had been asleep, comes running from her bedroom. She takes in the situation at a glance. "Come, we'll take him to the doctor in the car."

The big car noses through the stony maze of the shuttered shops and the streets empty except for a few strollers and a drunk sleeping off Saturday night. The doctor's door is locked. Luz Filomena strikes the steering wheel with her hand. "The hospital!"

The hospital stands on a back street, its courtyard enclosed by a blue wall. All the doors are open, but the lobby, of blood-red tiles, is empty. An orderly saunters in from a rear corridor, picking his teeth.

"Is there no doctor here?" Luz Filomena demands.

The orderly waves a languid hand toward the rear corridor, and, hurrying toward it, she sees, past an overgrown inner patio with a broken fountain filled with debris, that here are cubicles where patients are lying on iron beds.

"Doctor! Nurse! We have an injured child here."

Following, Nieves says nothing. She carries the heavy child inside her shawl; his tiny feet in sneakers, the laces dangling, hang down. Felicidad trots after.

Suddenly the corridor is crowded.

"An injured child."

An orderly puts Gabriel on a wheeled stretcher, where he lies without moving or crying, the blood pulsing gently out of the wound and down his neck. His shirt is stiff with it, and his pants and sneakers are spattered. In one clenched grimy fist he still clutches a coin.

Without speaking, the doctor writes a prescription for anæsthetic for an injection, and Luz Filomena hurries out to find a pharmacy. Gabriel's eyes are closed. With her shawl Nieves waves the flies from his face. Felicidad watches everything with wide-open eyes. In one of the rooms a young girl lifts her infant to the breast. In another, a bearded man lies motionless, his eyes fixed on the ceiling. In a third, a middle-aged woman is sobbing bitterly, embraced in turn by three girls, also weeping.

At last Luz Filomena returns, and a nurse wheels a cart over to Gabriel. With a wad of cotton saturated with disinfectant, she sponges the wound and three punctures on the other cheek. The gash is dark red, like bloody meat.

When the nurse unrolls a bundle of instruments, Luz Filomena sees the doctor coming down the hall toward them. Nieves sways on her feet. "I don't think I can see it," she mutters.

"I'll stay with him," whispers Luz Filomena. "Go with Felicidad and sit outside. Go."

When the first needle goes in, Gabriel gives a mewing cry, and his dirty fists fly up toward his face, but the nurse catches them. Luz Filomena holds his knees. Five times the needle goes in, followed by the stitches, and then the doctor walks away, leaving the bloody cloth still covering the boy. He has not even looked at Luz Filomena.

"Will he be all right?"

"The dog — was it wearing a blue tag?" the nurse asks as she applies a bandage.

"I don't know. Nobody saw. It was a stray."

"You can't bring it in for observation? Then the boy will have to have the rabies inoculation series. There is a certain danger. Some children have a fatal reaction."

"Ay, his poor mother."

"It is required by law."

In the lobby, Nieves sags beside Felicidad like a bundle of laundry.

"It is over?"

"Not yet. Inoculations — because of the dog."

"No, Lucha, no!" Nieves clings to her like a child. "I'm so afraid. Why Gabriel? Why not Felicidad?" Hearing the terrible words that have escaped her, Nieves clasps her daughter to her, covers her eyes with her shawl, and, for the first time, sobs uncontrollably.

After that one outbreak, Nieves, icy cold and motionless as a statue, stayed with her son. His hot little face, wizened with the fever, was always turned toward her, although his eyes were closed. He spoke only once: "Mamá, I won't go into the street any more."

After midnight, Luz Filomena, who had taken Felicidad home with her, returned with a priest. Nieves made no objection. Gabriel, allergic to the serum, died in the early hours of the morning.

7

ONLY TWO THINGS do not dwindle in importance: birth and death. The quarrels and jealousies of public men, the governments, the politics, the demonstrations, and even the wars, of which the fabric of history is patched together, are of no more consequence than the twittering of sparrows or the squawking of hens. And just as a birth can illuminate all of existence, briefly transfiguring an ordinary woman into an archetypal figure, so a death spreads the idea of death like a dark stain even to the most distant horizon.

Leaving her husband's house to return to Mexico City for a few days in the energetic world of commerce, profligacy, and ideology, Luz Filomena is chiefly conscious of a feeling of relief. In the house no relief or comfort is to be found. On the day of the funeral, Nieves had been composed, moving like a shadow over the rough cobbles on the long dusty walk to the cemetery, her face hidden in her black shawl. Behind her walked the three daughters, and Luz Filomena, seeing that shapeless antique figure, the mourning mother, understood that this was what Nieves had been becoming through all the years since she had first brought home that skinny little scarecrow with the pawprint birthmark, wild and timid as a desert animal. Despite schooling, pretty clothes, and all the blandishments of the wide world, throughout those years Nieves had been inexorably turning into this iconic figure of grief.

Until that moment Luz Filomena had believed, with the Señor Tío and Blanche Tole, that her fate was in her own hands, that her life was anything she chose to make it. In the presence of Nieves and these three children walking solemnly in the funeral procession, she felt her faith shaken.

Was there any such thing as controlling one's destiny? Did progress exist? Or was all humanity fastened helplessly to the wheel of need and blood, that wheel whose journey, no matter where the road turns, consists only of its own revolutions endlessly repeated? What would become of these children? How powerless she was to change anything. She felt a shudder pass over her, as of a shadow falling on her own grave, as she slowly followed the coffin, pathetically small. The procession was not long, although out of respect for the Señor Tío, more people came than usual for the burial of so young a child. Such funerals were all too common.

The day was hot and sunny, but at the grave the chill musty odor of the freshly dug earth reached into Luz Filomena's nostrils like the reek of death itself. This cemetery earth seemed the true earth of Mexico, an eternal charnel desert that could never blossom. Bones and salt tears were its only crop. Putting her black-edged handkerchief to her eyes, she looked at the mourning girls. Felicidad was sobbing noisily. Luz Filomena put an arm around her shoulder and thought, "She is suffering more than any of us." Afterward, back at the house, she gave Felicidad a handful of coins, and the little girl grinned up at her in surprise.

"Run along and buy some candy," she told the child, her thoughts scurrying like mice to the sugar skulls and coffins of the Day of the Dead.

"The priest said my brother is with the angels," Felicidad whispered, "but I am going to save some of the candy and take it to him in his box in the cemetery." It almost seemed as if the little girl felt her own place to be with her dead brother, because she had not been able to comfort her mother by taking his place.

Now, although she had intended to remain in the town at least until the Señor Tío's return, Luz Filomena found

the atmosphere of the house so oppressive that she decided
to travel as far as the capital with Blanche Tole. The big bus
of the Corceles de la Meseta travels fast, and on either side
of the road the country stretches rough and featureless to
the mountains. Today it seems grim and predatory, an un-
natural mother who would as readily destroy her children
as nourish them.

In the reclining seat next to Luz Filomena, Blanche Tole
says, indignant as always, "What upsets me most about the
child's death is that it was so unnecessary! The dog should,
of course, have had the rabies injection. What's the matter
with those people? It's free, isn't it? And if it wasn't wearing
a tag, the police should have picked it up and destroyed it –
not leave it running around in the street. Damn it all, what's
the point of the government having a decent public-health
program for once if everyone ignores it?"

Sadly, Luz Filomena shakes her head. "Ay, Bianca."

Luz Filomena does not doubt her friend's sincerity. She
too has tried to help people, even when they did not want
to be helped. And she has struggled on her own behalf to
escape the fruitless drudgery that was her only birthright.
On this bleak, rejecting earth, its only crop the bitter herb
of human suffering, of birth and death, is the struggle to
live itself the answer? It bequeaths to its children nothing
but a strength in their salt-tasting blood and in those bones
that outlast even grief, waiting and whitening in the dark
earth of the cemetery.

On the earth's surface, the struggle goes on. How many
forms it takes, always to be done over again, to be gone
through all over again, like the barely perceptible waxing
and waning of the moon, now to be seen through the windows of the bus, pale and thin against the darkening sky
like a sliver of bone on the rich velvet of a reliquary.

The coffee house of 17-century England was a place of fellowship where ideas could be freely exchanged. The coffee house of 1950s America was a place of refuge and tremendous literary energy. We hope such a spirit welcomes our readers in the pages of Coffee House Press books.